Clash of Faiths

The Paladins, Book 2

DAVID DALGLISH

BOOKS BY DAVID DALGLISH

THE HALF-ORC SERIES

The Weight of Blood
The Cost of Betrayal
The Death of Promises
The Shadows of Grace
A Sliver of Redemption

THE SHADOWDANCE TRILOGY

A Dance of Cloaks
A Dance of Blades
A Dance of Shadows (Winter, 2011)

THE PALADINS

Night of Wolves
Clash of Faiths

Prologue

The murmurs of the crowd were a welcome relief to Darius as he sat in the corner, his greatsword leaning against the wall beside him. The rest of the tavern seemed boisterous enough, the occupants receiving plenty of attention from the serving girl. He, however, had received only a single glare upon his request for water. Perhaps he should have ordered some ale along with his bread to win her over, but he would not pretend to nurse a drink forbidden to him. He was a dark paladin of Karak, and lost faith or not, he would still act like it.

"To Kaide!" one of the bigger men shouted, raising his glass. The rest took up the cry and then drank.

The name was familiar enough to Darius, though he wondered what the man had done to earn such drunken admiration. No doubt he'd filled their pockets with coin. Such lawless men in the North, they wanted money, alcohol, and women. Give them any of the three, and you were a better god than Karak or Ashhur would ever be …

"Temaryn, come to join us in our merriment?" called out someone at the bar.

Darius glanced at the door, and he felt his heart jump. Dressed in the black platemail of his order was another paladin, a longsword sheathed at his thigh and a heavy shield on his back. His hair was long and brown, perfectly matching his hazel eyes. Darius recognized him at once.

"Bloody Abyss," he muttered, looking for a way out of the tavern.

"You know I can't," Temaryn called back, approaching the drunkard with a grin on his face. "But I hear the mad thief left a pot of gold at our doorsteps. I take it every lesson I have ever taught will soon be thrown to the swine?"

"Course not!" said the drunk. "You'll get your share of tithes, but until then, we'll drink ourselves … hey, what's the matter?"

Temaryn was no longer paying him the slightest attention. Darius sighed and waved the other dark paladin over. His elbow bumped his greatsword, tilting it so the hilt lay across his lap. Just in case he couldn't talk his way out …

"I don't believe it," Temaryn said, pulling a chair opposite him and sitting. "What brings you here of all places?"

"I take it this is your assigned village?" Darius asked, avoiding the question.

"One of several. Never enough shepherds for the sheep, as I'm sure you know. The Stronghold has me run a loop here in the vale. Have you tried the bread yet? Nothing special, but they have some fantastic honey to go on top."

"Only butter," Darius said, his voice barely a mumble.

"Betty," Temaryn said, snapping his fingers. The serving girl came over and smiled. "Honey please, and some bread for myself."

"Of course," she said, giving him a smile Darius could only dream of getting.

"I don't know what they do to it," Temaryn said. "But you'll never get honey anywhere else in all of Dezrel like right here in Helmshire."

Darius felt his nerves relax, but only slightly. Temaryn remained at ease, the grin on his face never faltering. But his hand, though, stayed near the sheath of his sword. Habit, or conscious thought? The Temaryn he remembered from the Stronghold was an easy-going but faithful man. It could be either.

Temaryn leaned back in his chair, and he seemed to relax even more.

"So how are things in … what was that little place called? Durham?"

Darius thought of the two dark paladins and the priest that lay dead, slain by his hand at his false Tribunal.

"Fine," he said.

"Fine? That's it? I'm hearing stories of a thousand wolves held at bay by two paladins, amazing warriors of both Karak and Ashhur allied together against the entire might of the Wedge. Surely you don't mean to tell me the simpletons around here are *exaggerating* your fantastical exploits?"

There was something calculated about his laughter, something insidious about his question. Darius tensed, but he forced himself to remain calm.

"You know the people as well as I," he said as Betty arrived with a second plate of thick bread slices, along with a small cup filled with golden honey. Darius refused the offered honey, earning himself a frown.

"We're allowed few indulgences in our lives," Temaryn said as he drizzled the honey across his bread. "You should learn to accept them."

"If you say so."

Temaryn took a bite.

"You still haven't told me about Durham."

Darius shifted, his hand inching closer to his greatsword.

"Wolf-men crossed the river, not a thousand, only a few hundred. We stood against them, myself and the rest of the village. Nearly two-thirds of the people died, so I doubt too many are singing our praises."

"What of this paladin of Ashhur?"

Darius swallowed.

"His name is Jerico. Yes, he helped as well."

Temaryn fell silent for awhile, instead focusing on his bread. When the first slice was down, he sucked the honey from his fingers, then leaned back in his chair.

"I must admit, I was sent to Durham to find you. We'd heard a pretty outlandish story, and the Stronghold wanted me to look into the matter. Supposedly you had turned against Karak, and abandoned your faith. Needless to say, I found this hard to believe. I remember you from our training. The world would turn upside down sooner than you abandoning Karak."

A grim smile crossed Darius's face.

"To my shame, I must admit my faith in Karak is less than it was," he said. "But it is still strong."

"Good," Temaryn said, taking another bite of bread. "So was it difficult killing this Jerico?"

"No."

"No difficulty at all? Well, not much of a surprise—"

"He's not dead."

Temaryn put down his meal and pushed it away.

"So Pheus was right when he spoke of your friendship with the enemy? He wanted your head on a platter, Darius, and I'm not exaggerating by much."

Darius chuckled at the word 'enemy'.

"Yes, he did want that. That is why I killed him."

The humor finally left Temaryn's face. His hand closed around the hilt of his sword, and Darius did likewise.

"I never believed it," Temaryn said. "You, fallen? It made no sense. Even worse, slaying priests and dark paladins of your own faith? Nonsense, I thought. But Pheus vanished, as did Nevek and Lars. I hoped it wasn't you. You were never my friend, but you were an inspiration, an example of how much strength one could gain through the power of faith. Now look at you. Do you have any excuses, you wretch?"

"No excuses," said Darius. "Only a warning. Keep your sword sheathed. You were never as good as I, Temaryn. Never were, and never will be."

Temaryn stood, flinging his chair back. His shield and sword were in his hands, the blade consumed by dark fire.

"Karak has abandoned you!" the paladin cried. The rest of the tavern went deathly silent. "You are nothing without him, but he is at my side at all times. Draw your sword, Darius. Show me your lack of faith so I may kill you in good conscience."

Darius stood, grabbed his greatsword, and hefted it high above his head. No black fire consumed it. Karak's gift, a fire burning with strength equal to that of their faith, was absent from him. Seeing the mocking superiority in Temaryn's eyes, Darius tensed, knowing he had no choice. He didn't want to kill a brother in faith. But he would not die, either.

"Is that the proof you need?" he asked quietly.

"It is."

Temaryn lunged, his whole body extended to maximize the reach of his thrust. Darius smacked it aside, pivoted, and sent his sword crashing into his opponent's shield. At the sound of their collision, the rest of the tavern erupted with noise, people knocking over chairs and jostling one another to get out of the way. Such a battle was beyond them, and none wanted to be caught in the middle.

Temaryn took back the offensive. He knocked aside the table between them and closed the distance, his sword slashing and cutting with mechanical precision. There was no surprise to it, no fluidity. Darius's enormous sword positioned perfectly to block every time. With Karak's strength, Temaryn's sword hit his with a jolt, but he would endure. Temaryn had no innate sense of battle, no real talent for it. Darius, however ...

He stepped closer, feinted a thrust, and then swung for the dark paladin's knees. Temaryn's shield dropped, and though it blocked the swing, it gave Darius the opening he wanted. His elbow smashed into Temaryn's face, hard metal armor shattering his nose and splattering blood across the dark steel. Temaryn fell back, screaming, and Darius swung again. His greatsword slashed through the exposed underarm, tearing tendons and causing him to drop his shield.

Blood dripped to the tavern floor.

"It is not too late," Darius said. "Turn back. Don't make me add another sin to my burdens."

"Why?" Temaryn asked, his wounded arm clutched against his side. "If you know this is sin, then why?"

"Because I will not go to Karak as I am. I will not be a sinner for him to burn for an eternity. I must find a way to make amends. My faith will not go unheard."

"You're mad."

"And you're wounded. Go, now."

Temaryn lifted his sword.

"I will not run from you," he said. "I will not go to our god as a coward. You may have lost your faith, you may have turned your back upon Karak, but I will not. I will not!"

He charged, and Darius cut off his head with a single swing. As the body collapsed, Darius sheathed his blade and turned to the tavernkeeper.

"Take whatever price needed to clean this up," he told him, gesturing to the bag of coins tied to Temaryn's waist. "Give what is left to the next servant of Karak who comes."

The tavernkeeper, an overweight man who was sweating with fear, only nodded. Darius retrieved the head and put it back atop the body, using the weight of Temaryn's shield to hold it in place.

"The next you see me, I will not be the shamed, lost paladin," he whispered. "I will be a prince of Karak, a wayward son returned home. The Stronghold has twisted what we know of him. It has lied, and tricked me out of his blessing. My faith is strong. I will fight the chaos of this world, until Karak himself must speak my name and acknowledge my deeds. Pray no more brethren try to stop me."

He kissed Temaryn's forehead, placed a coin atop it to pay for his meal, and then left the tavern.

1

A sharp pain woke Jerico from his restless slumber. Delirious, he looked about, confused as to where he was and where he was going. The ground was in motion below him, but he felt unable to move. Tied? Not tied, he realized. He was in a net made of thick rope. That was a strange place to be.

"Why am I in a net?" he asked aloud.

Something hard struck his head, and he screamed. Colors danced before his eyes, and someone spoke, though the words were just a jumble compared to the ringing in his ears. Shaking his head, he tried to remember. He'd been traveling in the North, alone on the road, when he'd met an old man. Except it hadn't been an old man, he'd been ...

"Hey, Bellok, he's awake again."

Jerico twisted his head to stare through the gaps in the net. There was the older man, though not as old as he'd first looked. His hair was nearly white, but he walked with his back straight, and his skin wasn't wrinkled. He carried a staff in hand, and he waved it at Jerico.

"Another sleep spell and he might be out for a day or two. We best not risk it."

A dull tingle alerted Jerico to the uncomfortable position of his arm beneath him. He shifted, pulling his weight off it. The movement earned him a kick in the side, which his platemail thankfully absorbed. Worse was the pain that awoke in his once-sleeping arm, feeling like a thousand ants crawling through his veins, biting him.

"Would someone like to tell me what's going on?" he asked. His head pounded, and his stomach lurched with every bob of the net. From what he could see, the net was attached to a thick branch, carried on either side by two large men.

"Shut up," said the big lug behind him, kicking again. This time the boot connected with his head. The world spinning, he vomited. Much fell through the gaps of the net, but some stuck to the rope, and it smeared against his cheek.

"What a mess," the not-so-old man named Bellok said. "Don't worry, the sickness is just a residual effect of the spell. You'll feel fine soon enough."

"Wonderful," Jerico muttered. "Can I speak, or will I get kicked again?"

"Let him talk," Bellok said. "He's no wizard. His words can't hurt you."

"I just want him to stop moving," said the man at Jerico's feet. "He's too damn heavy."

"If I'd known I was going for a ride, I'd have taken off my armor."

No one seemed amused by Jerico's joke, which disappointed him. If he could get them to laugh, he could get them to like him. Instead he saw two brutes carrying him, neither cracking a grin, plus Bellok walking beside him. Jerico turned his attention to Bellok, figuring him the most talkative of the bunch.

"So ... Bellok, right? Where am I going again? I heard rumors of Kaide being a cannibal, so before anything else, please tell me I'm not about to be roasted over an open fire."

Bellok rolled his eyes and made a loud scoffing noise.

"Please, disgusting rumors with hardly a grain of truth. You will not be eaten, paladin, if hearing so puts you more at ease."

Jerico relaxed. Well, if he was going to die, at least it'd be in a normal, sane way. He really didn't want to meet Ashhur having just been someone's substitute for dinner.

The net shifted. What had been a flat dirt path below suddenly became heavy vegetation. They passed through bushes, the thorns scratching him through the net. He thought to ask his two captors to lift him higher, then thought better of it. The last thing he wanted was for them to decide to drop him even lower instead. Bellok vanished for a minute, then returned, picking burs from his robe. Wherever they were going, it was no longer on a standard road.

"Damn forest," the man muttered.

"So where is Kaide?" Jerico asked, more of his memory returning. Someone had spoken the name, and Bellok had confirmed it when he mentioned the cannibal rumor. If he interpreted his blurry past correctly, it had been Kaide who told the rest of the men to take him after they'd flung nets atop him and beaten him senseless. Of course, where they were taking him was another good question he doubted he'd get an answer to.

"Kaide is busy," Bellok said, a look of distaste crossing his face.

"Shagging some young tart," said the lug behind him. "Kaide can't turn down a little fun whenever we pass by a village. The lasses are practically flinging themselves at him."

"And someday one of those lasses will pull a dagger and claim herself a bounty of gold," Bellok said, glaring.

"Why would a girl do that?" asked the other guy carrying him. "You can't hump gold."

Well, thought Jerico, that explained Bellok's distaste; and also confirmed why he hadn't gotten a laugh from either of the two lugs. He knew donkeys with better senses of humor. And wit, now that he thought about it.

"So where are we going?" Jerico asked. "I hope not anywhere fancy. I must look a mess, what with the beatings and all."

"For someone an inch away from death, you seem in rather good spirits," Bellok said.

"Anything to stave off that final inch."

For once, Bellok smiled.

"You'll definitely be one of our more amusing captures, of that I'm certain."

Jerico fell silent. Well, this Kaide person had had captives before. He wasn't sure if that was good or bad.

"What happened to the other captives?" he asked.

The lug behind him leaned down, and his foul breath washed over Jerico.

"We ate them."

Jerico shifted his weight again, this time waking up his other arm and reigniting similar pain throughout the sleeping limb.

"Fantastic," he muttered.

He kept quiet as the minutes passed, spending the time in prayer with Ashhur. He didn't feel in any immediate danger, and his god gave little warning in his mind. Strange … the two captors carrying him were on the slow side, but they didn't seem particularly vile, beyond their smell. Bellok was intelligent, and appeared to take no joy in the situation. What had happened to the rest who had beaten him, though? They probably deserved a good walloping of Ashhur's mercy, and by god, he'd be glad to give it …

"We're here," Bellok said.

Jerico found himself unceremoniously dropped to the ground, landing hard on the twisted root of a tree. Biting down his cry, he pulled aside the net to stand. Both big lugs had drawn swords, and they pointed them at him. Jerico frowned. The men might be stupid, but they certainly took care of their weapons.

"Nothing funny," said one. "You run, we gut you."

"He won't run," Bellok said, gesturing for Jerico to follow.

Jerico didn't have the heart to tell him he was a bad judge of character. Instead he took in his surroundings, which were meager. Deep in the forest, it appeared Kaide's men had built a small cluster of homes in cleared areas of pine. They were small, a single floor with one or two windows and a door. They looked like a strong storm could blow them away.

"Cozy," Jerico said as Bellok led him toward the nearest of the homes.

"This is no time for joking," Bellok said, glaring. "If you value your life, you will listen and respond in an appropriate manner. Griff, Adam, you two guard the door."

"What if he tries something funny?" one of them asked. Whether it was Griff or Adam, Jerico hadn't a clue. Now that he was free of the net, the two looked like brothers, if not twins. Only the scars across their faces and arms failed to match.

"I may not care for Ashhur, but I know how his warriors behave. Don't worry. Inside, paladin."

Jerico stepped inside, Bellok following. The house was dim, lit only by the open window. A fire burned in the fireplace, the smoke drifting up a small chimney. In one corner was a bed, and lying atop it was a young woman buried up to her neck in blankets. A man sat beside her on a stool, his grey hair tied in a ponytail. There was something familiar about him, his hardened face lurking in some recent memory ...

"Kaide," Jerico said, remembering that man's face peering down at him, ordering the rest of the men to take him. "You're their leader?"

The man stood, tearing his attention from the woman. His eyes were red, and he looked like he hadn't slept in days.

"Forgive me for our first meeting," he said. "But you have no choice in this matter, and neither do I. Sandra is dying. I need you to save her."

Jerico approached the bed, making sure he kept his movements calm. Two long dirks hung exposed from Kaide's belt, their edges wickedly sharp. Jerico still wore his platemail, but unarmed, he'd be at a serious disadvantage if this Kaide knew at all how to wield those blades. Given his reputation, Jerico had a feeling he did. Trying to put such things out of his mind, he turned his attention to Sandra. Her skin was pale, her forehead beaded with sweat. Her hair was also grey, almost silver. No doubt if the color returned to her face, and her small lips smiled, she'd be beautiful. Removing his gauntlets, he set them on the floor.

"What is wrong with her?" he asked, pulling his gorget off his neck and putting it beside his gauntlets.

"She's been burning with fever for days," Kaide said.

"Sandra cut herself on some thorns," Bellok added. "Just regular cuts, but they've grown infected, and no matter what we do, it continues to spread. Check her arms, if you wish."

"You could do nothing?" Jerico asked.

"I'm good at destroying things, not fixing them," Bellok said, frowning.

"My sister is not a thing," Kaide said, a hard edge in his voice. Jerico found himself impressed by the sheer authority it carried.

"Quiet," he said. "Let me have a few moments of silence."

Jerico pulled down the blanket. Sandra slept in her shift, the short sleeves leaving her arms exposed. He took one in hand and turned it, looking at the marks. The skin around them had gone purple, the cuts themselves angry and red. No wonder she's overwhelmed with fever, he thought.

"Can you heal her?" Kaide asked as Jerico closed his eyes. The bandit's voice was soft, but had no hesitation, no quiver. This was a man who had seen death, and often.

"I can do nothing," Jerico said. "All I do is through Ashhur, and I assure you, nothing is beyond him."

He closed his eyes and prayed. He felt the closeness of his deity, and warmth spread across his hands. Clutching Sandra's arm, he pictured the healing light plunging into her skin, banishing the wounds, and pouring a cold fire across her fever. The woman shivered at his touch. A ringing sound filled his ears, then his prayers completed, and everything went silent. Dizziness overcame him, and he leaned against a wall to remain standing. Taking a deep breath, he opened his eyes to see the results.

Sandra still slept, but the cuts on her arm were but faded lines, soon to be nothing but scars. Already her skin had warmed in tone, and her sleep looked restful instead of pained.

"You did it," Kaide said, a smile crossing his face.

Jerico chuckled. "Not I, remember?"

Kaide waved a dismissive hand. Jerico stepped aside so the man could rejoin his sister. As he held her hand, Jerico plopped to a sit, still feeling dizzy. It sure didn't help that his entire body ached from the clubs that had beaten him, as well as the kicks from Griff and Adam. Bellok patted Kaide on the shoulder.

"I'll go tell everyone she'll be fine," he said.

Kaide nodded, and then the wizard left.

"So, Kaide," Jerico said, feeling like he should resume conversation. He wasn't sure what his current predicament was, and he wanted to get a far better idea. "I'm surprised you were here. Your, uh, men gave me the impression you were … occupied elsewhere."

A grin tugged at the corner of Kaide's mouth.

"There are twenty women who will readily claim to have bedded me tonight. Makes it difficult to track my whereabouts, wouldn't you think?"

"You keep this secret from your men?"

"Would you trust those two with any plan of yours?"

Jerico shrugged. Good point.

"Well, now that your sister is better, I feel like I best be going."

Kaide squeezed Sandra's hand, kissed her fingers, and then stood.

"No," he said, his hand falling to the hilt of a dirk. "I'm afraid that's not the case."

Jerico tensed. "I will tell no one of this place. Whatever you are, I will bear no ill will, especially since what was done to me was to save a loved one … even if you could have just asked."

"I fight a war," Kaide said, and he gestured toward Sandra. "And in a war, you don't let go of any advantage. Griff, Adam, get in here."

The two stepped inside, surrounding Jerico.

"Oh, hey boss," said one. "Didn't know you was back."

"I am," Kaide said. He stared at Jerico, watching, waiting. "Please, take Jerico to his room, and make sure the locks are tight. He's to be fed and well-treated."

"No beatings?" asked the other.

"No beatings."

"Much appreciated," said Jerico.

They each grabbed him by an arm and led him from the house. Nearby was another building, this one noticeably lacking any windows. The two lugs shoved him inside and slammed the door shut. He heard a loud thud, most certainly a bar of some kind locking into place. The door had a single slit, and the room dimmed as someone stood before it, grinning.

"We'll treat you like royalty," he said, laughing. "So take your royal shits in that corner with the bucket, and you'll get your royal meal at sundown. That's when we'll take the bucket."

The slit closed as something pressed over it, sealing Jerico in darkness.

"Well," Jerico said, scratching his neck. "I think I preferred the wolf-men. Thanks, Ashhur."

He leaned against the wall opposite the bucket, closed his eyes, and slept.

<hr/>

Darius stood in an open field, facing the west. The sky was an ugly yellow and filled with clouds. They growled with thunder, and lightning streaked pale blue across the horizon. Wind blew against his bare skin, for he was naked as the day he was born. He wished for his sword and armor, but didn't know where they were.

Darius, cried the thunder, its rumbling forming an unearthly voice, cold and deep. He saw a face in the clouds, and it was the face of his god.

"Karak," Darius said, falling to his knees. "Forgive me my failures, but my faith is only for you!"

The face laughed. No mirth. No amusement. Only contempt.

Strong of faith, yet without wisdom, and full of doubt. You bow to me, but then ignore my words. You swear allegiance, and then disobey. You are nothing to me, Darius. Once you were, but no longer.

"No," Darius cried as the wind howled, stealing away his voice. "I will not be abandoned! I will not die as I am! I have served you, every day I have served you!"

Then obey!

The clouds formed a funnel, which struck the far distant plains. It grew, wider and wider, until it stretched for miles. The sound of its approach was like that of a thousand dragons roaring in fury. Before it, Darius felt small, pathetic. He begged and wept for salvation, but the swirling grey monster tore into him, shredding his skin and striking him with stones. His feet left the ground, and then he was flying, flying ...

His screaming woke him in his bedroll. At some point his thrashing had knocked his blankets aside, and he shivered in the cold night air. Above him, the stars twinkled through the naked interlocking branches. No clouds. No storm. Nearby, his campfire had died down to embers. Rolling over, he meant to add kindling and wood, but then it burst to life. In the newly granted light, he saw a dark-robed man sitting beside it, his legs crossed beneath him.

"Nightmares, Darius?"

Darius startled, and he grabbed his sword despite knowing it would do no good. He'd struck this man before, only to watch the steel bounce off pale skin as if it were made of stone. Velixar, Karak's prophet, laughed as if he were privy to his thoughts.

"Is that how you work?" Darius asked. "By interfering with my dreams?"

"At times, yes," said Velixar. "But not tonight. Do you think I would take an interest in you without reason? Karak watches you, and he gifts you with his divine presence. You should be honored."

The prophet poked at the fire with a stick, as if he had suddenly forgotten Darius was there. Darius watched him for a moment, trying to decide if he lied or not. The man's face, pale, thin, and lit by red eyes that glowed with fire, changed with every passing second. By the time he turned around and smiled, he appeared a new man, his cheeks wider, his lips thinner, and his chin longer. The eyes remained the same.

"What did our Lord say?" asked the man with the ever-changing face.

"He wished me to obey."

"As I said you would one day."

Darius glared.

"He said to obey him, not you. You do not speak his will. You've led us astray, all of us. You're a relic, a man lost in a different time."

Velixar resumed poking the fire with his stick, talking all the while.

"Serve Karak through serving me. Even children can understand this concept. You have felt Karak's fury, yet you still deny you failed him? Still believe that you know his true heart and will? You amuse me, Darius, as much as you disappoint me. Sit awhile with me by the fire."

Reluctantly, Darius stabbed his sword into the dirt and did as he was asked. He swore the air grew colder around the prophet, and he felt his insides twist at their proximity. As he sat, Velixar pointed to the fire, where he'd drawn several runes with his stick. The flames swirled, deepened, and then suddenly opened onto a vision of another place, one also filled with shadows and fire. Standing amid a great chasm of men, his obsidian armor gleaming, was Temaryn.

He wielded a flaming sword in one hand and a whip in the other.

"Do you see?" Velixar asked. "He rules in the Abyss, purifying the wretched given to our lord. I will not judge you for sending him to Karak, for his soul is secure, and he is in his place. You, however ..."

Darius could not look away from the horrific image. This was the future awaiting his Order? Temaryn looked pleased enough, and he lashed the sinners with his whip while crying out for repentance and obedience. The vision changed, and he saw a hundred things that he could not remember the moment after they passed, only feel the lingering terror and anguish. Through it all, the dead marched, sang, and burned with clockwork precision. True to his god, the Abyss was a place of order above all things.

And then he saw himself, up to his knees in a lake of fire. He was naked, and bleeding from many open sores. A man in shining armor towered over him, his very skin wreathed in flame, his movements trailing shadow. Removing his helmet, this tormenter looked up from the vision and straight into Darius's eyes. It was him, only stronger, more faithful. Darius cried out, and he tore his eyes away from the sight. Kicking his foot, he scattered the fire, ending its heat. In the sudden silence, a distant wolf howled.

"You must choose," Velixar said, his voice barely above a whisper. "Only two fates await you, and you have seen them both. Pretend to wisdom, or bow to those with understanding. You will cleanse, or be the tormented. There is no other fate left."

Velixar stood, stepped into the shadows of the forest, and then was gone. Darius sat there, feeling drained. Everything else he'd seen was already fading from his mind, all but that last image of himself—both versions. They stared up at him, one in pain, one lost in ecstasy. He could almost imagine them pleading for him to make the right choice ...

Darius fell to his knees, bowed his head, and cried tears to his god. He begged for wisdom, he begged for guidance, but all he heard was the silence and the distant cry of a wolf.

2

Jerico stirred as blinding light hurt his eyes. Blocking it with a hand, he tried to decipher who stood at the door.

"To your feet, paladin," he heard Kaide say.

Jerico stood, groaning as he did. His platemail groaned along with him. He wished to oil it down, but could not. He refused to even take it off. So far the other men hadn't demanded it of him, and he didn't want to risk losing it now. As he stepped out, still shielding his eyes, he realized it wasn't daylight that hurt him, but burning torches at either side of his door.

"What is the hour?" he asked.

"The stars are out," one of the two lugs grumbled behind him, still guarding the door. "What hour you think it is?"

Jerico turned and smiled at the yellow and red blob that his eyes showed.

"Ever so helpful, Griff."

"It's Adam."

"Sorry, can't see your scars too well."

It seemed like Adam grinned, but then a sharp pain struck Jerico's throat. He collapsed to one knee and coughed.

"Take his armor," Kaide ordered as Jerico fought to regain his breath. "I don't want it turning a blade should we need to subdue him."

Jerico tensed, and he almost resisted. In the end, he knew it was pointless. Half-blind, hungry, and disorientated, he would prove no challenge. Lifting his arms, he let Adam tug at the straps, pulling his armor off.

"Careful," he said. "You'll dent it."

"It seems dented enough by your own travels," Kaide said as the breastplate thudded to the dirt. "You should feel better not carrying that around, anyway. Now follow me."

Jerico's sight was finally coming around, and he glanced about the forest dwellings. He saw the light of fires burning in several homes, and a few more outside in a ring. The sound of laughter met his ears, so he figured it couldn't be too late into the night. The amount of people he heard and saw surprised him. At least a hundred formed this motley bunch.

"Did something happen to Sandra?" he asked as they returned to where the woman had been kept.

"Just be quiet," Kaide insisted. He pulled the band from his hair, releasing the ponytail. Shaking his hair free, he sighed and put a hand on the door. "Behave yourself, and respond kindly. Sandra has woken, and she wishes to thank you."

He pushed it open, then gestured for Jerico to enter. As he did, Kaide followed and shut the door behind them.

Already Sandra looked worlds better. Her arm was bandaged, its linen clean. She smiled at their entrance, confirming Jerico's earlier suspicion about her beauty. Her room was lit by a fireplace, but it had dwindled down, allowing a chill to enter. Kaide took to tending it, as if he wanted no part of the proceedings.

"Are you the paladin?" Sandra asked. Her voice was thick with the northern accent, and it masked how tired she clearly was. Jerico nodded, trying to make sense of things. He'd been dragged from a windowless prison to be thanked? Would he be sent back afterward? Hardly seemed an appropriate reward, but Kaide had further plans for him, that was obvious. Would Sandra know any of it? No, of course not. She'd been out at the time of his capture, and he had a feeling her brother had not filled her in.

"I am," Jerico said, bowing.

"Thank you," she said, smiling. She sat up, tugging her blanket so it remained wrapped tight about her. "I doubt I'm worthy of such a noble gesture, though."

"I bow to all beautiful women," Jerico said, glancing at Kaide. Sure enough, he was glaring death, which made it all worthwhile.

If Sandra was flattered, she kept it in check.

"If you say. Please, sit by my bed. None of the men here, my brother included, are much use for conversation. Too dull, too focused. They haven't seen the world. Have you?"

"I think you should get some rest," Kaide interrupted. "The hour's late, and—"

"I have slept for days," Sandra said, glaring. "Please, give us our privacy. Or do you think a paladin of Ashhur will murder me in cold blood the same day he saved my life?"

Jerico found himself liking the woman more and more.

"So be it," Kaide said, nearly growling with rage. He flung another log into the fire, not caring that he scattered it. Jerico waited until he left, chuckled, and then took Kaide's place at getting it roaring.

"Don't judge him too harshly," she said. "He has a temper is all."

"I don't think that's all," Jerico said, gently pushing the errant log aside so he could layer on more kindling.

"I take it he blindfolded you before bringing you here?" Jerico laughed.

"If you consider being dragged here unconscious in a net as blindfolded, then yes, I was."

Sandra fell silent, and Jerico berated himself for his sharp tongue. It certainly wasn't her fault. The fire finally going strong, he stood and closed his eyes, enjoying the warmth. His room had felt like ice when he'd been awoken. Dread filled his stomach as he thought of the coming night, without blankets or a fire.

"He's keeping you in the windowless room, isn't he?" she asked quietly.

"He is."

"No fire, no blankets, and no bed?"

Jerico looked her in the eye.

"You seem familiar with your brother's accommodations. I hope those who came before me all deserved the same treatment."

Her neck flushed red.

"That was uncalled for," she said. "I wished to thank you, and hear of the Citadel, the waters of the Gihon, and the peoples in the lands beyond Mordan. Yet you'd call me a jailor, instead?"

Jerico felt petty, but he was tired, grumpy, and unable to stop himself.

"You're sister to one. And forgive my lack of tales, for my prison's not as comfortable as yours, Sandra."

She sat erect in her bed, her jaw trembling with anger.

"Get out," she said.

Jerico rolled his eyes. There were a million ways he could have handled the situation better, but of course, he'd screwed them all up.

"Please, I'm sorry, it's just …"

"I said out. Kaide!"

The door opened so fast Jerico wondered if the man had been pressing his ear against the other side. He held his dirks in hand, and seemed disappointed that he had no reason to use them.

"Let's go," he said, grabbing Jerico's arm and pulling. "Back to your room."

Jerico bowed once more to Sandra and then allowed himself to be led back to his prison. When inside, he shivered against the wall, enveloped once more in darkness. He tried to sleep, but could not. Even with how slow time crawled, it was not long before the door burst open.

"Yes?" Jerico asked.

"Off your ass," Adam said. "Come on, now, hurry!"

With a blade pressed against his back, Jerico was pushed back into the night and toward another building. The door was opened, and they shoved him inside. Within was a bed, a fireplace, and a slender window too small for him to crawl through.

"Courtesy of the woman," Adam said, shutting the door. He heard the sound of locking, then whistling as Adam wandered away. Jerico checked the bed for lice or fleas, and found none. Impressive.

"Well, Jerico," the paladin said, finding it disturbingly easy to talk to himself given his lack of company. "It looks like you're not that terrible at talking to women after all."

He knew that was false, of course, but it was nice to pretend otherwise.

The following day passed full of tedium and boredom. Jerico ate his meals when they were brought to him, and filled the rest of his hours with exercise and prayer. He wanted both his muscles and his faith sharp should any chance at escape present itself. So far his captors didn't seem to have any intention to kill him, so he remained patient. It wasn't like he had anywhere else to go, not with dark priests and paladins scouring the North.

"There's a disturbing thought," Jerico muttered, thinking of Kaide selling him to someone from the Stronghold for a nice sack of gold. Or would he be worth only silver? Questions he'd never get adequate answers to. His personal pride wanted Karak's servants hurling entire treasuries at people to bring him down, but that seemed unreasonable. Maybe just a few thousand gold. That'd at least be something worth bragging about.

Not that he had anyone to brag to. Adam and Griff alternated guard duty, broken up by the occasional third man named Barry. An impatient and ill-tempered man, Barry was actually the worst of the three. The twins, as he'd discovered, would at least joke around, however poorly, when he spoke to them through the hole in his door. Barry only shouted for him to shut up.

"Must you always be talking in there?" the man once asked around midday.

"I'm praying," Jerico replied.

"Then pray into a pillow or something. Tired of hearing it!"

Jerico spent the next hour praying directly in front of the door, and his lamentations were loud and heartfelt. He even prayed for Barry's soul, and only the iron will of a paladin kept him from breaking into laughter at the angry shouting *that* caused.

Come nightfall, he heard only silence. He wondered if they'd left him without a guard. No one answered his occasional question. Through the window, he saw the occasional person milling about, nearly all of them male. He wondered if Kaide recruited only unmarried men, or if they kept their families somewhere else, presumably safer. Jerico added that to the list of other questions he expected to never receive an answer to. The best information he could get out of Adam and Griff was their last name: Irons.

When the stars were at their fullest, the door opened without a single knock for warning. Sandra stepped inside, then closed the door behind her. Jerico sat on his bed, feeling ragged and dirty. It'd been days since he bathed, and despite the moderately improved living conditions, he was still not the cleanest. Brushing a hand through his hair, he smiled, then remembered to bow.

"Kaide still thinks you will run," she said, as if struggling to think of something to say. "Will you?"

"Not going to lie. If I thought I could, I'd already be gone."

"You haven't tried breaking down the door, or digging through a wall. You've made no effort to escape. You speak in blusters."

"How do you know?"

She smiled at him.

"Because you're a paladin. That's just not what you do, is it? Or have the stories I've heard all been a lie?"

Jerico shrugged. "Depends on what stories."

"What about the one with you and the wolf-men?"

The paladin groaned.

"That one made it all the way up here?"

Sandra seemed intrigued by his annoyance. She sat in a chair beside his small fire, shifting her skirt to the side. Her dress was thick and cut high, practical for the rough terrain surrounding the area.

"I think all of Mordan will be talking about that one for a while, though the paladin's name has changed several times. But I still think it is you."

"And why's that?"

"I've seen your shield."

Jerico shrugged. Seemed pointless to argue it.

"I wasn't alone," he said. "And the men with me fought bravely, many dying to protect others. We fought a few hundred wolf-men, killed most, and chased the rest off. Meanwhile, more than half the town died. It wasn't some epic victory, not the true version of the story, anyway."

Sandra shifted in her seat.

"I liked the one I heard better. It described you as a man with hair made of fire, and a shield of pure light. You would point it at your enemies, and the light itself would strike them down. I heard not a man died, not a woman or child touched."

Jerico thought of the horrors he'd seen, and the many graves he'd dug.

"I'd rather talk of something else," he said.

"Like what?" she asked.

"Oh, why your brother's keeping me captive. That might be a fun story to hear."

Sandra rolled her eyes.

"That's something *I'd* rather not talk about, either," she said.

"Forgive me for pressing the issue anyway."

Standing, Sandra looked away for a moment, as if collecting her thoughts.

"What do you know of Lord Sebastian Hemman?" she asked. At Jerico's shrug, she continued. "Not many know anything about him outside our lands. By law, he rules much of the North. He draws his wealth from our fields, our mountains, and the sweat of our brow. When Kaide could take it no longer, when he was given no choice, he gathered his friends and struck back."

"Fascinating," Jerico said, trying not to sound condescending. "But what does this have to do with me?"

"You'll see soon enough," she said. "Kaide's off chasing rumors of Sebastian's knights traveling the road through the forest. You'll be needed when they return."

"Why did you come to talk to me?" Jerico asked before she could exit the door. "Is it guilt?"

A sad smile marred her beautiful face.

"I'm here because I wish things were different," she said. "I'm here because I want you to know we are not butchers, thieves, and cruel people."

"You kidnap, rob, and attack men loyal to the king," Jerico said. "Your brother breaks hundreds of laws. Oh, and his thugs beat me with clubs. Forgive me for not warming up to him."

Sandra left, refusing to argue the point. Jerico slammed a fist against the wall when she was gone.

"Help me out, Ashhur," he whispered. "I don't have a damn clue what I'm doing."

An hour or so passed, a disturbing silence compared to the previous day and night. All commotion had died down. Sandra said Kaide had gone after some of Hemman's knights, and he must have taken the entire camp with him. If there was ever a time to escape, it was now.

"I want no part of this," he said, leaning against the door. In the dark, he could see little through the slit. Still, there appeared no guard, and he heard no nearby noises. Putting his hands against the door, he tested the lock's strength. It budged, but only a little. Stepping back, he kicked it once, twice, and then slammed his shoulder against it. The wood groaned, and the noise seemed thunderous in the quiet. Preparing another charge, he just barely stopped in time before impaling himself on the tip of a spike that pressed through the door's slit.

"I must admit," Sandra said from the other side. "I'm disappointed."

"Move aside, Sandra. I won't be kept prisoner."

The metal tip remained.

"I have a bow as well," she said. "Even if you kick down the door, you won't escape. I've learned plenty from my brother, Jerico. I know the vital spots to kill a man. You aren't leaving, not until he gives you his blessing. I'm sorry."

Jerico sighed, and he slumped down into the chair Sandra had occupied. It seemed absurd, knowing he'd have to subdue a single woman to make his escape. But armed with a spear and a bow, she was quite capable of killing him. More importantly, he'd have to hurt her to protect himself, and that was something he wasn't willing to do. To strike at a woman, just because he didn't like his current sleeping accommodation? Hardly the actions of the champion of mankind he was supposed to be.

"Very well," he said, wondering how in the world he'd ended up in such a predicament. "I'll behave."

"Good."

The tip vanished, and he saw her eyes peer at him through the door. He could tell she was smiling.

"You better not tell anyone about this," he said.

"Everyone who will listen. Don't worry, you'll even make it outside in this tale, before I wrestled you to the ground and beat you unconscious with my bare hands. Should earn a few chuckles around the campfire."

Jerico laughed, deciding he easily liked her most of all his jailors so far.

To prepare himself for bed, Jerico knelt and began his prayers. Barely a few minutes in, he heard distant shouts. Stopping, he went to the small window and tried to see. Torchlight flickered through the trees, and a crowd of men appeared, walking along a path. A couple veered his way, and he stepped back from the window. A short while later, the door opened, and in stepped Kaide. A wicked bruise bled across his brow. Blood stained his clothes.

"Outside," he said. "There isn't enough room in here. Shit, it's bad, Jerico. I hope you can handle it."

Jerico gestured for Kaide to lead the way, and then followed the outlaw. Around a large, central campfire he saw ten bodies, lying in a circle to keep them near its warmth. They all had various wounds, some minor, some severe. Jerico circled them, taking in the damage. Surrounding him were the rest of the men, talking quietly to themselves and watching him intently.

"You assaulted armored knights," he said, turning to Kaide. "All of these are by swords. They injured themselves breaking the law, and attacking innocent men."

"Innocent?" one of the ruffians asked, and two others had to grab him to keep him from attacking Jerico.

"Will you heal them?" Kaide asked.

"Should I?"

They exchanged a look. Jerico didn't know what to think, or what to do. Part of him just wanted to alert Kaide to the reality of his situation. In the end, it didn't matter. The bandit leader stared him in the eye and called his bluff.

"If you are who I think you are, you would never sit back and watch a man die. Do not argue with me, risking my men death, just to waste my time and satisfy your pride. Do your duty, paladin."

Jerico's stare hardened, but then he turned away. Kaide was right. It didn't matter if these men were murderers or thieves. He would not watch them suffer needlessly. Circling the fire once more, he sought out the worst of the wounded, and knelt beside a bearded man with a cut across his belly. The man held his fists pressed against it, keeping his entrails from spilling out.

"Let go," Jerico said, putting his hands atop his fists. "Close your eyes, relax, and let go."

The man reluctantly obeyed. Jerico closed his own eyes and gave himself to Ashhur in prayer. Light shone from his fingers at their contact, pouring across the skin. It knitted the flesh together, healing the wound. Done, Jerico stood, took a deep breath to steady himself, and then went to the next.

Two of the ten were already dead by the time he could go to them. Several others had mortal wounds, wounds he sealed with his faith. The rest, with minor cuts or broken bones, he treated last. Torn muscles he mended, and broken bones snapped together amid the cries of their owners. At last, Jerico collapsed to his knees and stared into the fire. Cold sweat dripped down his neck, and his head pounded. Nearby, Sandra went from man to man, wrapping what remained of their cuts with bandages, and giving slings to the men who'd broken arms or fingers so they might not strain their tender appendages.

"Well done," Kaide said after chatting with a couple of the men who had, only minutes before, been at death's door.

"Thanks," Jerico said, still not opening his eyes. He felt ready to vomit, though he didn't know if he had anything in his stomach to empty. Something slapped his shoulder, and he opened an eye to see a waterskin. He took it and drank, then turned to the side and vomited it all back up. Coughing, he prayed for the dizziness to stop. At Durham he'd handled worse, but that day felt centuries away. He was tired from the road, nursing bruises and desperate for food and drink. An empty shell, he lay on his back and stared at the stars through the naked canopy of branches.

Kaide sat beside him, acting unbothered by the vomit nearby. He took his own drink from the waterskin, and then offered it a second time. Jerico weakly waved it away.

"They were ready for us," Kaide said. His voice was soft, and it lacked the hard edge it'd had before. "Only reason we lived was because we came at them from both sides. Don't think they realized just how many have sworn to my name. Still, they wore heavy armor, like yours. Half my men have nothing but clubs, tree branches. Do you know what it takes to bring someone down with only that? Gods damn it all, the gore we left inside that armor ..."

He fell silent for a moment, took a drink.

"Left twelve men back there, dead or too far gone to survive the trip back. Couldn't even bury them. Didn't have the time. Could only burn them."

"I'm sorry," Jerico said. He wasn't sure if he was, but it felt like the right thing to say.

"You need to be there with us," Kaide said, still not looking at him. "My sister's told me who you are, what you've done. Those knights ... you could have taken out half of them by yourself. And my friends, my wounded ..."

He wiped at his eyes, quick, subtle.

"There would have been time for them."

Jerico rolled onto his knees, waited for his stomach to settle, and then stood. Ashhur help him, was this all he would ever be good for? Healing the wounded and presiding over the dead?

"I don't know what god you worship, if any," he said. "But I will pray over your dead, if you would allow it."

Kaide nodded.

"It'll do a lot of the men good. You have my blessing."

There were about sixty of them gathered around the two graves, nearly all sporting cuts and bruises. Four men had taken turns shoveling, and another had whittled down stakes to place above them, with a single letter cut into the wood to mark their names. When the bodies were in place, and the dirt ready to fall, Jerico stood before them. He felt their eyes watching him, felt their confusion, anger, and doubt.

"Let us pray," Jerico said, beginning the burial ritual.

When he was done, they shoveled the dirt back into the grave, and Kaide led Jerico back to his room. When he laid down on the bed, he heard muttered talking, then nothing. Curious, Jerico forced himself back up and to the door. A slight push was enough to confirm what he thought. The door was unlocked. Stay or go, he wondered. What is right?

In the end, he returned to his bed and slept. Ashhur had guided him there for a purpose. He had to believe that, for all other possibilities frightened him, left him alone and adrift in the land of Dezrel. As sleep came to him, he vowed to find out the reason, and attack it with all his might. But his dreams were not of duty, or vengeance, but of Sandra, smiling at him with her sad smile.

3

For several days Darius saw no sign of Velixar, and this heartened him greatly. He always felt his lowest in the prophet's presence, as if he stood before a standard that he could never hope to achieve. Velixar had the faith of a man who spoke with deities, while Darius could only wander the wilderness road, glad for the moments of silence.

On the third day, he heard the heavy sound of hoofbeats coming from the south, and he stopped to await their arrival. They might be bandits, knights, or riders from the Stronghold. No matter what, he would neither run nor hide, only face them in the open and meet any challenge issued.

Ahead, the road curved, and around that curve came six knights in worn platemail. They were not of the Stronghold, that was obvious enough. Darius saw the symbol on their shields, that of a yellow rose, but didn't recall its significance. He raised his hand in greeting, expecting similar in kind. Instead the horsemen encircled him, their swords drawn.

"Identify yourself!" their leader shouted.

Darius chuckled, wondering if he was supposed to be intimidated.

"I am Darius of the Stronghold, paladin of our mighty god Karak. And who might you be?"

The knight lifted the visor of his helmet to reveal his face. His hair was dark, and he had a scar running along the bridge of his nose.

"Sir Gregane, knight of our lord, Sebastian Hemman. We've been tracking a group of bandits, and they struck not far from here."

"Do I look like a bandit? Put your swords away, before I am offended."

A nod from Gregane, and the men sheathed their blades.

"My apologies," said the knight. "We have been ambushed many times, and feared you were part of another."

"Bandits and rebels are men of chaos. You should remember that, knight, before you ever question the allegiance of a paladin of Karak."

As Gregane nodded again, a second knight leaned in and murmured something to him in a low tone.

"Very well," Gregane said, turning his attention back to Darius. "Our lord has been seeking one of your faith. I ask that you ride back with us to his castle."

"And if I refuse?"

Gregane glanced at the rest of the riders.

"I would strongly recommend against doing so," he said.

Darius sighed.

"Very well."

They had no spare horse, and could not carry two with how burdened each of them were with their heavy armor. One dismounted and offered Darius the reins.

"Her name's Esme, after my wife," said the knight. "Treat her well. She has a temper."

"The horse, or your wife?" Darius asked as he adjusted the saddle.

"Both," he said with a grin.

"I'll send a rider for you, Isaac," Gregane said. "Stay off the road. Bandits might still be near."

They rode north, Darius in the center of the formation. Most kept to themselves, for which the dark paladin was thankful. He had no desire for conversation, not while he pondered the reason for his audience. Never before had he been to the Castle of the Yellow Rose, and it didn't seem that Lord Hemman requested him by name. No doubt he wanted some sort of religious guidance, though why no members of the faith would be with him at the castle seemed odd. Perhaps they were all hunting their new favorite prey…

The thought reminded him of Jerico, and he wondered how the paladin fared. Had he fled north, as Darius had suggested, or turned about to head south? What of the dark paladins, had they found him yet? He hoped not. Deep down, Darius still felt the bloody conflict might end, that it was no true war. But the various lords, ladies, and kings would turn blind eyes to conflicts of faith, so long as it did not disrupt their people or bathe their streets with blood. Darius knew his brethren would be too careful for that.

They emerged from the forest about an hour later, the castle not far in the distance. Its walls stretched out for a mile beyond the castle itself, sealing in several pastures with crops and cattle, along with numerous wells. Darius eyed the walls. They were short, and made of dark stone. Ladders would easily reach the top, and battering rams would make quick work of their gates, but that wasn't their point. They were for holding off uprisings of peasants and raids by bandits, who lacked even the most basic of siege weaponry.

The castle was equally unimpressive, save for one thing. As Darius entered through a gateway, following the knights along a beaten dirt path, he saw the great rose painted across the face of the castle. It drooped to one side, and a single petal fell, twirling in an unseen wind. Vines grew across the face of the walls, adding texture to the painted petals. Darius couldn't begin to imagine how they painted it, nor kept its color vibrant. As a defensive foundation, it was basic, square, and crenellated along the tops.

Sir Gregane announced their arrival, and the castle's doors were flung open. Young boys appeared, leading away the horses once the knights dismounted. Darius kept an eye out for priests and paladins of either faith, but saw none. If lucky, he might appear before Sebastian, offer some vague advice, and then be gone.

"Follow me," Gregane said. "But first, your sword."

"I go nowhere without it, not even before kings and queens. I will not disarm myself before your lord, especially when I am brought here as a guest."

The other knights tensed, but Gregane seemed unoffended.

"Very well. Keep it sheathed on your back. I cannot promise you safety otherwise."

Darius gestured for him to move along. They stepped into a short hallway, past several doors leading to the lower and upper floors of the castle. Then they were inside the grand room, with rows of tables for feasting at the foot of a single throne made of stained oak. A man sat on it, thin and wiry, with his dark hair reaching far past his neck. Flecks of gray shone in the black.

"Sebastian Hemman," Darius said, not waiting for introductions. "I am Darius of the Stronghold, faithful paladin of Karak, and I bring with me his blessing."

Sebastian sat ramrod straight in his chair, and at the announcement, he bowed his head slightly and gestured to a table that had a meager offering of food.

"You may eat and drink, if you'd like," said the lord. His voice was soft, calculated.

"Perhaps when business is done," Darius said. He remained standing, even when the other knights bowed in reverence. Darius would bow to no one, nor call them lord; his kind served Karak and Karak alone. "I have never been fond of empty pleasantries, nor stalling words to feel out another's true thoughts. Let me state this plainly: I have come because you have summoned me. Let me know why, so I may perform my function, and then go on my way if I so choose."

"Impatient words," Sebastian said. "But I've found your kind often is. Sometimes I think Karak sends those gifted with golden tongues to his priesthood, and the blunt muscle to the Stronghold."

Darius grinned.

"No one will ever accuse me of a bronze tongue, let alone golden. I have my sword, and that is enough. Tell me, Sebastian, why am I here? Are there no others of the faith to counsel you?"

"We once had a priest here, but he has left, with business he swears is most urgent." Lord Hemman took a drink of wine from a cup at his side, still in no hurry to move things along. "But the seventh day approaches, and we have no one to administer the offerings, nor have we had for several weeks. Would you preside over this for my people tomorrow?"

That was it? Darius tried to contain his temper. He'd basically been kidnapped and brought before their lord, all so he could perform a function even the youngest of the faith could handle?

"If that is what you require, I accept, but I have matters I must attend, and cannot stay long."

"Yes, of course. Now that that is settled …"

Sebastian clapped his hands, ordering everyone out. Gregane opened his mouth to protest, but the lord silenced him with a glare. The servants vanished, shutting the door behind the knights. When they were alone, Sebastian stood, and he seemed to visibly relax.

"Forgive me that tedious business," he said, eagerness bleeding into his voice. "It has been weeks since any worshipper of Ashhur was here, but I thought it best to hide the reason for your arrival just in case. Castle walls have ears, after all, and mine are no exception."

"I see," Darius said, though he didn't. If not for the morrow's service, why was he here? A ball of lead formed in his stomach, for of all the ideas he had, none were pleasant. The lord moved to a door behind his throne, and he opened it with a key wrapped around his neck. Taking a nearby torch, he stepped inside, beckoning Darius to follow. Heart in his throat, he did.

The air was heavy, and the floor damp. They descended into a dank dungeon, the only sound that of the flickering torch and a distant dripping of water. At the bottom of the stairs was a cell, and inside that cell was an older man strapped upright to the wall with iron.

"Who is this?" Darius asked, already dreading the answer. "Answer me."

"It is a brave man who will make demands in a lord's dungeon," Sebastian said. "But that is your nature, I suppose. I have always been a faithful supporter of Karak. Ashhur appeals to the peasant folk, the simple minded who need promises of greatness in death, who need a doctrine that elevates them as equals to gods. Karak knows better. It is Order the world needs, a king, his lords, and their subjects. That is the divine sequence."

"Enough," Darius said, wishing to hear no more of the man's simplification of a doctrine he knew better in his sleep. "Answer my question."

"His name is Pallos," Sebastian said, opening the cell door. "My men captured him along the road, and have brought him here. Before he left, Laius, one of your priests assigned to be my counsel, spoke whispers of a war. He told me of the Citadel's fall, and of the great cleansing that sweeps across Dezrel. Of course, I would not dare steal from you a rightful execution. Besides, if the priests of Ashhur received word, they might make my life … difficult."

Darius stepped into the cell, his throat dry. The paladin's name was so familiar. Pallos … that was it. Darius had promised Jerico that he would warn Pallos of the silent war should he encounter him again. It seemed such a warning was no longer necessary. The older man looked up at him, his eyes still lucid despite the thinness of his body and the darkness of his cell.

"Leave me," Darius told Sebastian. "I wish to have words with this man, of things you'd best not hear."

"Of course." The man bowed and stepped back, keeping his torch high so its light might still shine on them both.

"Who are you?" Pallos asked, his voice cracking.

"My name is Darius … of Durham."

At the name, Pallos tensed against his shackles.

"Have you turned against me?" he asked. "Has the entire world? I warned Jerico, but did he listen? He counted you his friend."

"And he still does," Darius said, his voice dropping to a whisper. "I had not the heart to kill him. He lives, Pallos, at least last I saw him. The world is dangerous, though, so I cannot know for certain."

Pallos's mouth dropped open, and he looked torn between hope and distrust. Darius knew the man had no reason to believe him. Everything he said could be a trick, or a cruel torture to be later revealed as a lie.

"I don't believe it," he said at last. "I thought for certain … Karak would call you to kill him."

"He did."

"And you refused?"

Darius sighed. This was hardly something he wished to go over again, for the wound still stung.

"Yes, I did."

"Praise Ashhur," Pallos whispered.

"I doubt Ashhur deserves much praise. His paladins are being butchered day by day, and now I find you here, chained to a wall and starved half to death."

Pallos's eyes twinkled, but he refused to argue.

"What now?" the older man asked.

Darius glanced back at the lord. What now indeed? Here he was, before a man declared to be his enemy by the highest members of his faith. Could so many be wrong? Even Karak's very prophet insisted the followers of Ashhur were an enemy, and that Darius would only know Karak's strength when he embraced that reality.

He looked to Pallos. The man's skin hung on his bones, and his fingers shook without ceasing. Sweat dripped from his head—or was it water from the ceiling? He tried to decide what was right. He thought to pray to Karak, but he suddenly felt afraid of his deity. It wasn't that he would receive no answer; in fact, the opposite. What if Karak called him to kill? What if Darius still stubbornly clung to an image of his god that was untrue?

"You will die, no matter what I do," Darius whispered. He pulled his greatsword off his back and held it in his hand. "They will leave you here, starving, chained, until another priest or paladin comes along. They will torture you, make you scream and beg. They might even force you to denounce your faith, to cry out in pain that all your beliefs are a lie. I cannot save you, Pallos, but I can grant you death here, now. It will not be done in anger. I will lessen the pain as much as I can."

"Your blade," Pallos said, acting as if he never heard a word. "It does not burn."

"My faith is still strong," Darius said. "Will you accept my mercy?"

"You hold faith," Pallos said, a smile covering his face. "I do see that, but is it in the god you think you serve?"

"Enough," Darius said, his voice rising. "Karak is my lord, my protector, my strength. I offer you this in kindness. Give me an answer. I will not murder you, only save you. Let me hear the words."

The old paladin let his head fall.

"I hear you," he said. "Do what must be done. I know what fate awaits me in the hereafter."

Darius stepped to the side, closing both hands around the hilt of his sword. He heard Pallos whispering a prayer to his god, and the sound knifed through his heart.

"I do no wrong," he whispered. "I perform no sin. In this, I take no joy."

He swung. His greatsword cleaved through Pallos's neck and struck stone on the other side. As it did, Darius saw a black flame burst from his sword. It terrified him, and he refused to think of it, and locked it far away inside his mind.

"A single cut," Sebastian said, grinning. "Well done, Darius."

Darius did not bother to contradict him.

"I must go find lodging," he said, distracted.

"Nonsense." The lord beckoned him to follow. "You will stay with me here, in the castle. I'll not have you go seeking an inn, as if I turned away an honored guest. Consider it another part of my service to Karak."

"If you wish."

The keeper of the dungeon, a heavy-set man who had remained hidden in the shadows, stepped out at their departure. Darius glanced back once, saw him unhooking the body for burial, and then looked away.

Valessa hated the wilderness. She felt exposed without the comforting crowd of the city to blend in and vanish. Every noise seemed louder, every footfall breaking a twig or leaf. When in cities, though, she yearned for the outdoors, to be away from prying eyes that were ever watchful. In truth, she was generally unhappy wherever she went, though she was reluctant to admit it.

"Must he have fled to the North?" she asked, ducking her head underneath a branch. The top of her hood rustled its leaves, and she felt several break off and fall upon her and her horse.

"Wouldn't you, if you knew the might of Karak chased after?" asked her companion, a smaller, slender woman named Claire. They both wore heavy gray cloaks over their outfits, plain clothes hiding tightly interwoven leather armor.

"I wouldn't bother running," Valessa said. "I'd at least be willing to face my Tribunal and die with honor."

"Dying in betrayal to Karak has no honor, no matter what manner of death."

Valessa drew a dagger and stared into its perfect sheen. True, there was nothing honorable about the deaths they brought. They were the gray sisters, and they killed in secret, and in silence.

Claire pulled back her hood and shook her blonde hair loose.

"Day's warm," she said. "The most in two weeks, at least."

"Just means winter's about to arrive in force," Valessa grumbled.

"What, you hate winter now?" Claire laughed. "I've always thought blood looks beautiful spilled across white snow. That, and it's easy to blame a death on the frost, if we're careful enough, and don't use a blade."

"Keep your wire and poisons to yourself, Claire. My knife is enough to … *shit!*"

She hadn't been paying attention, only trusting her horse to follow the road. At the last moment, she saw a thin coil of rope hidden beneath an unnatural pile of leaves. Yanking on the reins, Valessa reared her horse back, trying to avoid it, but it was too late. The rope snapped, its knot closing in on her mount's front two legs. The horse shrieked as its body was brutally jarred to one side, its legs unable to properly balance. Valessa leapt clear to avoid being crushed underneath. She rolled, spun, and drew a blade in each hand, her eyes already surveying the area for assailants.

"Show yourself!" Claire called out, still mounted. So far, no one revealed their presence.

"An unwatched trap?" Valessa asked.

"We're not far from Sebastian's castle. Bandits have been making his life miserable, from what I hear. This may be just a nuisance."

Valessa kept her body in a crouch, ready to move at a moment's notice. Her curved daggers never wavered in her hands. Her horse continued to make noise as it struggled to stand. Tiring of the distraction, Claire pulled out a small crossbow that had been attached to her belt and fired. The bolt sunk into the horse's throat. Valessa watched, knowing it would not take long for the lethal poison to end the creature's pain. Its breathing turned heavy, its head fell, and finally they could hear.

The forest was eerily silent around them. If there were critters about, they remained low and hidden. Valessa felt the hairs on her neck rise, and she knew she was being watched. But from where?

"My horse can bear two," Claire said, spinning her mount in place so she could check all directions. "We can race along, or flee back south."

"Traps might be set in either direction," Valessa said, her voice low. She took a careful step toward Claire, then another. What were they waiting for? Two women, riding alone, and they were smart enough to treat them as dangerous prey? Whoever these bandits were, they were either cowards, or too intelligent for their own good. Valessa certainly hoped for the former.

"Stay still!" a man's voice shouted to her right. She spun. A man camouflaged with mud stepped from around a tree. He held a bow in hand, an arrow notched but not pulled at ready. Another man followed behind him, holding a heavy club.

"Only two?" Claire asked.

"Whose service are you in?" the man with the bow asked.

"Karak," Valessa answered.

"No, your lord."

"We have no lord but Karak," she said, starting to lose whatever patience she had. The men stepped closer, and she spaced out the distance between them. She could be at their side in a second, two at most …

"So you're not with Lord Sebastian?" the man with the club asked.

Claire rolled her eyes.

"No," Valessa said. "We're not."

He jabbed the other with his elbow.

"I tolds you," he said. "We just killed them ladies' horse!"

"How was I supposed to know? They was riding along like they was messengers!"

"You two are bandits, I take it?" Valessa asked. The two men, seeing that she did not appear angry, calmed.

"We're warriors of Kaide Goldflint, not bandits."

The two gray sisters exchanged a look.

"Is that so?" Valessa said. "Pardon me. I would hate to insult such mighty men. Please, put your weapons down. I would feel terribly upset if one of us was hurt through another ... accident."

The closer one lowered his bow, but the other kept a tight grip on his club. He was staring at her daggers, she realized. She certainly didn't look the helpless maiden. Realizing this, she abandoned her stance, and a smile crossed her face, an easy, well-practiced mask.

"We're ladies of the south," she said. "My weapons-master taught me a few things, but I can only do so much with these little blades. Hate holding them, honestly. Fighting is for the men."

"Aye, it is," said the bowman. He approached, and he bowed clumsily. "Forgive us. We meant no harm to your horse. But we're fighting a war, and sometimes accidents can hap—"

Valessa rammed her elbow into his throat, silencing him. Her first slash cut the string from his bow. Her other hand sliced in, opening his belly. A twirl, and both daggers ripped gashes across his chest. Mouth hanging open, he stared at her, dumbfounded, as he died. She heard a twang, followed by a sharp whistle, and knew Claire's crossbow was at it again. Turning to the man with the club, she found him slumped against a tree, a bolt sticking out of his left eye. He tried to say something, but the poison was already working through his body, paralyzing him.

Valessa wiped the blood from her daggers and sheathed them. Checking herself, she found she'd stepped in where her horse had shit itself upon death. Muttering, she scraped her boot clean on the road, then kicked the man she'd killed.

"When we find Darius, he doesn't die immediately," she said, frowning at her boot. "I want time to make him suffer."

Dark laughter cut through the forest, and both women startled at the noise. Standing in the shadow of a tree, his eyes shimmering, was a pale man in black robes.

"I know you," Claire said, and the chill in her voice was frightening. "You're the one who claims to be Karak's prophet; whom the priests call Velixar."

The man smiled, his face gradually changing as he did. Valessa tried to act calm, but before her stood a legend. Her knees suddenly felt weak, and her heart pounded in her chest. The man with the ever-changing face, the Voice of the Lion, was truly before her?

"I have heard stories of you," Valessa said, offering a low bow. "Though I never thought I would be gifted with your presence."

"Few consider my presence a gift."

"Then they are not loyal to Karak."

Velixar smiled, but his eyes were analyzing them both, peering into her in a way that left her feeling naked and uncomfortable. Valessa looked to the dead bodies nearby, and for some reason felt embarrassed by them.

"Why are you here?" he asked.

Claire started to answer, but Valessa cut her off. She would not lie about her mission, not to one as ancient as the prophet.

"We hunt for the failed paladin known as Darius. We are to be his executioners."

"No tribunal?"

"He had his tribunal," Claire said. "He killed them. We need no further testimony, no trials. The Stronghold has cast him out and declared him a traitor."

Velixar seemed amused by the words, but that amusement never touched his eyes. They burned like fire, and Valessa struggled to look away.

"Then you two are gray sisters, the priests' ghosts in the night. I should have known the honor of a Tribunal would be beyond your handling."

"We do the work of Karak, same as you," Claire snapped. The ire in her voice stirred something inside Valessa, and she shook her head as if struggling to wake from a dream.

"Will you help us?" she asked. "We've traveled from Mordeina, and the North is vast. Darius might hide anywhere, and it is best we deal with this soon, before he might further damage the faithful."

"Help you?" Velixar laughed. "No, sisters, I will not help you. I recognize your cloaks, your garb, and though you may not remember it, I dipped inside your dreams last night. That is why I am here. I come bearing a command: leave Darius to me. He is mine to teach, and to discipline, as I desire."

"We can't abandon our mission," Claire said. She was openly glaring now, and Valessa tried to figure out why. She knew little of the prophet, only vague stories, many of them surely exaggerated. To be ordered away from a kill was disheartening, true, but Claire looked like she'd been ordered to commit treason.

"You are disobeying the order of your god," Velixar said, his deep voice rumbling.

"The priests have decided otherwise," Claire said, and that was then Valessa remembered. The Council of Stars.

"You have no authority over us," she said. She felt her palms sweating as she clutched her daggers. "The priests gathered, and High Priest Multhar—"

"Multhar was a coward and a fiend who beat children for his sexual perversions," Velixar said. His hands shook with rage. "None of you hear the words of Karak. None of you have stood in awe of his majesty and strength. I was there, sisters, one of the first men ever given life from the dust. I was there as he battled Ashhur, when he was so close to victory. Our god gave me eternal life even as he was imprisoned by the elven whore. He gave me this mantle, and I have carried it for *centuries*, you damn fools. Do you think I care about the opinion of a single man, or his councils?"

Claire's horse backed away at the violent fury of his voice, and Valessa felt a desire to fall to her knees and beg for forgiveness. But she was stronger than that, and her own fury rose up. No one dared challenge her faith.

"It is no matter," Claire said. "You are a prophet, indeed, but the words of prophets are slippery, and often confused. The Stronghold, in its wisdom, has demanded Darius's death, and we shall deliver it. If you disagree, then go to our High Enforcer and let him hear your anger."

"Slippery?" Velixar asked. "Confused? Hear me, the time comes when war will bathe all of Dezrel, when even the faithful will be tested. Angels and demons will bleed from the sky, cities will burn, and I will be made a prince over the army of Karak. This future approaches, and is closer with every breath you take. Do you think, in that newly come age, you will stand before me and declare me false? Declare me *confused?*"

Valessa stood tall, and despite the hammering of her heart in her chest, she spoke calmly, and with authority.

"In that day, we will serve Karak, no different than we do now. We will not bow to you. You are not Karak, even if you speak for him. We have heard Karak's words in our own way, and we will do our duty. A man slaughtered fellow members of the faithful, and we will bring vengeance upon him. Do not try to stop us."

Velixar shook his head. All his anger was gone, replaced with a mixture of sadness and disappointment.

"You two are faithful," he said. "That I can tell. It is a shame you have no wisdom. I have given you my warning. Darius is mine, and mine alone. Interfere, and I will bring the wrath of the Lion down upon you, and we shall see which of us Karak truly favors."

With that, he was gone, vanishing in a blur of shadows that trailed to the sky like dust. Claire's horse neighed, seeming more at ease after the prophet's vanishing.

"Bravely spoken," Claire said, guiding her horse over and offering Valessa a hand. She accepted it, feeling as if she were waking from a nightmare.

"I pray we did no wrong," she said.

"Do not worry. He's a phantom of another age. The world has moved on, though I fear he still lingers in past wars and sacrifices."

"If you say so," Valessa said, sitting behind Claire atop her horse. "Still, he is powerful. I have no doubt about that. And I doubt your poisons will do anything more than make him mad."

"Well," Claire said, gently nudging her horse onward. "In that case, we can always cut off his damn head. I don't care how immortal he thinks he is. No one lives through that."

Thinking of his gaze, and those eyes which burned like fire, Valessa didn't feel quite so certain.

4

After Jerico finished his morning meal, Kaide stepped inside without knocking. He leaned against the wall beside the door, his arms crossed, eyes hard. Jerico pretended not to notice.

"You didn't try to escape," Kaide said.

"Was I supposed to?"

"You can't be happy with my keeping you here. To be honest, I'm not happy about it, either. But you saved the life of my friends last night. If given the choice of keeping them alive, or letting you loose, well … surely you understand my choice?"

Jerico sighed.

"Do you think me an idiot?" he asked. "I can see what is before me. I understand, and I don't blame you. Doesn't mean I like it, or that I think you're in the right. There are other ways."

"Then why did you not try to flee? Did you know I posted a guard in secret?"

Jerico shook his head.

"No, Kaide. When I leave this place, I will leave in daylight, standing tall, and my shield upon my back. Not like a thief. Not like a coward. Besides … I have nowhere else to go."

Kaide looked away, and he seemed lost in thought. Jerico returned to his bed and sat upon it. He missed his armor, particularly his shield. Still, vulnerable as he was, he would not act it before the bandit leader. Ashhur was still with him, no matter the state of the rest of the world. With him, he would show no fear.

"You are a paladin," Kaide said suddenly. "Your word is law to you, correct?"

"I don't lie, and I don't break promises," Jerico said. "Just not my style."

"Then fight for me," he said. "Give your word you won't leave, and you can be free to roam the forest. You alone could frighten many a knight, and to have you there in the conflict ... those I left behind, they might still be alive."

"No," Jerico said, shaking his head. "I won't lift my mace for you. But I will promise to stay until I have your leave, if you'll let me come and go as I please. You have my word."

Kaide didn't look happy, and his frown looked strong enough to cut stone.

"Some of my men worship your god," he said. "They want you to counsel them, give one of your ... whatever, sermons. Will you?"

"You heard my demands."

"Fine. Give me your word."

Jerico stood and offered his hand.

"I will stay, offer my wisdom, and help keep your men alive. All I ask is that you listen, and lie to me not, as I will not lie to you."

"Your kind can sense lies," Kaide said. "Is that not what the stories say?"

"They do."

Kaide took his outstretched hand and shook it by the wrist.

"Then you know I speak truth. Help me, protect those I care for, and you will be no prisoner."

"Excellent," Jerico said, a smile spreading across his face. "I was about to go insane cramped in here. When do I get my shield and armor back?"

Kaide opened the door and stepped out.

"I don't remember saying anything about that," he said, and winked. Jerico opened his mouth, closed it, and realized he should pay more attention to the deals he made.

"Never was much for politics," he muttered to himself.

Kaide led him to the main campfire, where the rest of the men were eating. Some gave him a strange look, but most appeared happy to see him. Given how many of their wounds he tended, Jerico figured he at least deserved a bit of common courtesy.

"Jerico has agreed to help us, of his own volition," Kaide said to the men. "He is no prisoner, and I expect you all to treat him like one of our own."

"He gonna fight?" one of the burlier ones asked.

"*Can* he fight?" asked another familiar voice. Jerico turned and saw Adam glowering nearby.

"A mace and a shield," Jerico said, grinning at him. "That's all I'd need to get that nose of yours broken in a more appealing direction."

The rest laughed, and Jerico was surprised to see Adam did, too.

"Took nearly six of us to take this bull down," he said, smacking Jerico across the back. "And that was with a damn net to help. Better you with us than locked in a cabin like an unfaithful woman."

"Jerico will only be using his healing arts," Kaide said, sounding none too pleased about it. He glanced at Jerico, and there was a spark of hope in his eyes. "Though maybe he will help in your training. There's only so much I can teach you sods, and my training is nothing compared to what the Citadel offers."

"Offered," Jerico said.

Kaide gave him a funny look, then shrugged.

"Either way, he'll be giving his sermons soon, though it will be up to him when—"

He stopped, and Jerico followed his gaze. A horse approached from the forest path, though its rider was not the soldier or bandit he expected. Instead it was a young boy, still a year or two from having the first hairs sprout from his chin. He rode to the fire and hopped down before the horse was even settled.

"Kaide!" he cried, rushing up to the man.

"What is it?" Kaide asked, a deathly seriousness coming over him. "What's wrong?"

"It's Beth," the boy said. "She, she …"

Kaide put his hands on the boy's shoulders, holding him still as tears overwhelmed his ability to talk. Jerico stepped beside him, and whispering a prayer, put his hand on top of the boy's head. Calming emotions poured into him, so when Kaide spoke, he had rapt attention.

"Listen to me, Ricky," he said. "Take a deep breath, right now, and then let it out. Good. Don't look at anyone else, just at me. Tell me what's wrong. No tears. Just talk."

Ricky sniffed, but he stared ahead, and did as Kaide asked.

"Beth got bit by a spider," he said. "First Ma thought it was nothing, but it made her veins red like a strawberry, and it went all the way up her arm. Ma says we should've cut it off, but we didn't, and she's getting worse, and her hand, it's … it's …"

"Enough," Kaide said. "You've done fine. Tell me, wasn't there a paladin there? Gahal, or something like that?"

"He's gone," Ricky said, shaking his head. "We got no one. That's why Ma sent me to you. She said she wants you there for Beth, before she … goes."

Kaide patted the boy on the head, then stood. He looked to Jerico, who didn't even need to think before answering.

"You know I will," he said.

"Your sister ain't going anywhere," Kaide said, motioning for another of the men to come take care of the boy as well as stable the horse. "You understand me, Ricky? Rest up, and eat something."

He hurried toward the southern edge of their camp, and Jerico followed.

"You gave me your word," Kaide said as they entered a small stable with only three horses.

"I plan on keeping it, too."

"Can you ride a horse?"

Jerico grabbed a saddle and set it atop the largest of the three.

"Learned plenty at the Citadel," he said, feeling a sting just saying the place's name. "Yes, I can ride, and ride fast. How far is Beth's village?"

"Place called Stonahm. Six hours ride, four if we push the horses to their limit."

"I'd rather not kill one creature trying save another," Jerico said as he mounted.

"My Beth is no creature," Kaide said, fury in his eyes.

"Forgive me," Jerico said, stepping back. "Then we'll see just how strong these beasts are. My shield, where is it?"

Kaide shook his head.

"I'm traveling alone with you on horseback while leaving my little fortress. Let's not test my trust any further than I already am. Now ride, you bastard, and try to keep up."

He kicked the sides of his own horse and bolted down the path as if the hounds of the Abyss were at his heels. Jerico whispered a soothing word to his own mount, offered a prayer to Ashhur, and then was off in chase.

The hours passed, Kaide in the lead, Jerico trailing. They left the forest within the first half hour, bursting onto open plains like wanted men ... which in a sense they were, though Jerico derived little pleasure from the comparison as he thought of it. Now without a path, Jerico relied on Kaide to lead the way. The hooves thundered below them, and Jerico prayed no animal holes or hidden rocks tripped either of them. As the day wore on, the plains turned to hills, and they wound through their centers. The grass, which had been thick and tall enough to scratch at the bottoms of his feet, steadily shrank. When the hills ended, Jerico saw the first of the farmland.

"There?" Jerico shouted, pointing to a distant village.

"Beyond," Kaide shouted back.

A shift of direction, and they found themselves on a worn dirt road. Following it, they crossed between the fields, all low-cut and freshly harvested. They stopped at a stream to let their horses drink and catch their breath.

"Would that we could ride all day without stopping," Kaide muttered.

"It has to be done," Jerico said, knowing it would be little comfort. "How old is Beth? If she's big enough, she might fight off a bite, unless the spider was a black fiddler."

Kaide put his back to him, instead tending to his horse. When he said nothing, Jerico pressed on.

"Who is she, Kaide? Why do we ride?"

"Beth's my daughter," he said. "I'll speak no more of it."

Jerico opened his mouth to ask a question, thought better of it, and instead tended his own mount.

They rode in silence, the only sound that of their horses hoofbeats and heavy breathing. In the distance, Jerico caught sight of a white line of smoke just behind a cluster of hills that broke the monotony of the fields. He glanced over and saw Kaide's eyes staring at it, and he knew Stonahm was near. The road led them there, and even if it didn't seem possible, Kaide urged his mount ever faster. Bandit and paladin, they thundered into the dirt streets of the village.

"Where's Beth?" Kaide shouted at no one in particular. Already a crowd gathered, and it was obvious to Jerico that Kaide was respected, if not revered. He bit his tongue and resolved himself to say nothing. He would not judge, only listen and learn.

"Here, Kaide!" shouted an older man, his hairline receding and his blue eyes showing hints of a murky white.

The people parted, and the two followed the old man into a thatched hut. Inside was dark, and smelled heavily of herbs and incense. Jerico fought the urge to cough.

"She's been bitten," said the man, gesturing to where a young woman slept on a bed, blankets pulled up to her neck. "I'm sure Ricky told you as much. I've drained it best I can, but it's beyond my healing. I'm sorry, Kaide. I tried, I really did, but sometimes it seems like the gods seek a life, and nothing can stop them from taking it."

"No god will steal her from me," Kaide said, kneeling beside his daughter. "Beth? Beth, can you hear me?"

"Hasn't stirred for at least an hour," the old man said, carefully settling into a chair near the bed. "Sleeping more than me, even. Oh, hrmph, where are my manners."

He stood and offered Jerico his hand.

"My name's Kalgan. Pleasure to meet you ...?"

"Jerico," he said. "Of the Citadel."

"Citadel?" Kalgan glanced back at Kaide. "Is it ... did you truly find a healer for her?"

"I did," Kaide said, standing. When he looked to Jerico, his face was a cracked mask, the emotion behind threatening to break loose at any moment. "Do your duty, paladin."

Jerico stepped close to examine the girl. She looked twelve, maybe thirteen. Her hair was dark, the same color Kaide's must have been before the early gray took over. She had a round face, large cheeks, and a hint of a scar underneath her chin.

"Which arm?" he asked as he pulled down the blanket.

"The left," said Kalgan.

He needn't have asked. The fingers of her left arm were black and blue, the veins a violent red as they snaked up to her shoulder. All across the arm were small black lesions.

"Black fiddler," he muttered. Behind him, Kaide swore.

"I thought as much," Kalgan said, sighing. "I feared to speak it aloud, though you may think me foolish. Didn't want to make it true by saying it."

Jerico chuckled at the superstition as he tried to remember details of such a bite from his time at the Citadel. His lessons on healing magic had been sparse, and mostly focused on a single detail: if his faith was strong, and the injured still alive, then anyone could be saved. Whether she would keep her arm, however, was another matter entirely
...

"Kaide," he said, making sure he kept his voice calm. "I may ask you for something you will immediately refuse. I ask you to think on it instead, and to trust me. Can you do this?"

"What are you talking about? Just tell me."

"I said will you do it?" He turned, and the stern look on his face was enough to make Kaide back down.

"For her," Kaide said. "Please, just ... save my little Beth."

Jerico closed his eyes, and as he whispered the first of many prayers, he touched Beth's arm. To his sensitive mind, it was like touching fire. He gritted his teeth and endured. He'd healed broken bones and bleeding wounds the size of fists. He would not be defeated by the poison of a spider. Light shone from his touch, and it spread. Jerico dared look only once, but it was enough to make him shudder. The light faltered.

"What's wrong?" Kaide asked.

"Quiet," Jerico said through clenched teeth.

The healing magic danced through the flesh of her arm, like long trails of light in his mind's eye. Everything he touched was burdened with death, tainted black. He tried to flood it with light, to give of his strength to power the healing. As with everything, there had to be sacrifice, and it came from him. He gasped at the effort. Broken limbs were just thin mendings of bone. Cuts were malleable skin. This, though, this was giving life to the dead.

Sweat poured down his head, and he heard ringing in his ears.

"Kaide," he said, his voice labored. "I cannot do it. It's been too long. Her arm's begun to rot. She'll live, I swear on my life she'll live, but I must remove it."

"Her arm," Kaide said. "But ... no, she's just ..."

Jerico glanced back to see Kalgan putting a hand on Kaide's shoulder. The bandit leader swore again, then looked away.

"Do it," he said. "But I will hold you to your oath."

"Give me a knife."

The work was fast and brutal. Jerico had no time for subtlety. The arm was like an anchor pulling her body toward death. Fever and rot, slowly crawling upward. He cut it off at the elbow, freeing her from it. Blood spilled across the bed. When the arm was removed completely, he pressed his hands against the stump and begged to Ashhur for strength. He should have cut the arm immediately, he knew, but he'd had to try to save it first. That attempt had sapped much of his energy, so that even breathing proved difficult. Now he needed just a little bit more, for some venom remained past the cut, like an embedded thorn.

"Not for me," Jerico prayed. "Not for me. For her."

He never heard it, never felt it, but Kaide gasped behind him, as did the old man. Jerico counted to ten, then opened his eyes. Beth still slept, but already color was returning to her body. What little red that had shown in her veins was gone. Taking the severed arm, Jerico wrapped it in a bloody blanket and handed it to Kalgan.

"Burn it," he said. His hands shook as he held it. "Burn it, and remember why it had to be done."

Without a word Kalgan slipped out of the room. Unsure if he could stand, Jerico shoved himself to a sit adjacent to Beth's bed, giving Kaide room to go to her.

"Beth," Kaide said, taking her remaining hand and kissing her forehead. "I'm here. Daddy's here. You can sleep, but you aren't going anywhere on me, do you hear? Daddy couldn't ... Daddy couldn't take it. You're all that's left, all right, so you stay strong."

Kaide collapsed into the chair Kalgan had sat in, no doubt remaining at her side during much of her illness.

"Was she left-handed or right?" Jerico asked, his eyes closed and his head leaning against the wall.

"Right," Kaide said, and he laughed mirthlessly. "Should I thank Ashhur for that small favor?"

"How about the big one? She lives, she breathes, and she'll love you as much now as she ever did before. An arm's just an arm."

They heard commotion from outside the hut. From his time in Durham, Jerico knew that in such a small village every member would be aware of Beth's brush with death, and no doubt word of her survival would spread like wildfire. If they had anything to spare for a feast, they'd surely prepare it now.

"You're right," Kaide said after a lengthy pause. "Forgive me."

"Nothing to forgive."

Kalgan stepped back inside, and he looked much relieved to have the severed arm gone.

"I must say, Jerico, I usually scoff at the little things others insist are miracles from the gods, but your arrival is surely one such miracle. To have one of our paladins die, only for another to come in our hour of need ..."

"Die? Who died?" Jerico asked.

Kalgan glanced at him, raising his bushy eyebrows.

"He'd been with us only a few weeks. Young lad named Galahall. Did you know him?"

Jerico shook his head.

"Younger than me, most likely. How did he die?"

"Troublesome, that, but I've always said the dealings between gods should be left to the gods themselves. He fought a paladin of Karak, over what I'm not sure. I can only assume it was important."

Jerico bolted to his feet, losing his balance as he did. Kaide caught him, looking bewildered.

"What's the matter?" he asked.

"The dark paladin," Jerico asked. "Is he still here?"

"Kren? Yes, why?"

Jerico looked to the thin door of the hut, imagining the commotion outside. In the minutes that had passed, surely everyone in the village had heard the same story, that of a paladin coming and healing sick little Beth. A paladin of Ashhur ...

"We need to go, now," Jerico said, but it was already too late.

The door was kicked open, and there stood a man in the black armor of Karak, a roaring lion painted in yellow across his shield. His sword was still sheathed, but his hand rested upon it, ready to draw. Jerico stood to his full height, his right hand leaning against the wall to keep himself steady.

"You're young," Jerico said, for he thought of nothing else to say.

Kren sneered. He was a handsome man, his brown hair falling far beyond the reach of his helmet. Shadows of a beard grew about his chin.

"You come without weapon, and without armor?" Kren asked, surprised. "Was this a ploy, or a disguise? Surely you have not cast aside your faith if you can heal the bandit's girl. Such sad sport is this."

"I don't need either to handle a young pup like you," Jerico said, wishing he felt as bold as he sounded. "But this is a house of healing. Would you disgrace your hosts by spilling blood across this floor?"

"Enough!"

Kaide stepped between them, and he glared at Kren.

"What is going on here?" he asked. "What madness draws you to challenge a man you have never met?"

"This has nothing to do with you, Kaide. Step aside."

"Not until I hear something that makes some damn sense."

Kren drew his sword, a serrated blade that swarmed with dark fire. He pointed it at Jerico's throat.

"Their time is at an end," he said. "Karak has called for war. What paladins of Ashhur are left are few. I will not lose such an honor as to have slain two of their kind."

"This man has saved the life of my sister, and my daughter. Consider the honor denied."

They glared at one another, the tension thick enough to cut. Jerico knew what was about to unfold, and he could not allow it. With such close quarters, and without any armor, Kaide didn't stand a chance. He would not save Beth's life just for her to wake to her father's slaughter. The dark paladin was preparing for an attack. No time left to think, Jerico glanced at the walls. The hut was old, and appeared used only as a house of healing. Its walls were thin, aged boards with rusted nails. Swallowing his pride, he grabbed Kaide from behind, flung him to the side, and then dove the other way.

His shoulder hit the wall first, followed by the rest of his body. The wood cracked, and boards tore loose. Jerico rolled along the grass, clenching his teeth against the pain of a dozen cuts across his exposed arms and legs. Pulling out of the roll, he spun to see Kren giving chase. The gathered crowd shouted their disproval, for they knew Jerico must be the stranger that had come to heal Beth. As Jerico watched, several men tried to block Kren's way, only for one to be cut down, and two others shoved aside. Despite their anger, the villagers were unarmed men and women. What could they do against a man fully armored and wielding a blade of dark flame?

Jerico glanced down at himself. Good question. What could *he* do unarmed and unarmored versus such an opponent? Still, no others would die for him.

"Let him pass!" Jerico shouted. "I stand here on open ground. Face me, dog of Karak!"

Reluctantly the crowd relented, and Kren burst forth, running as fast as he could in his armor. Jerico tensed. Mobility was his only defense. Even with superior faith, he had no item to project that power through, negating any other potential advantage he might have had.

Kren tried to gut him without slowing his charge, no doubt trusting his armor to protect him should they collide. Jerico twisted, avoiding just in time. Kren's feet skidded across the ground, and he changed directions before Jerico could dodge again. Blood splashed over them both as the blade wounded his chest. Crying out in pain, Jerico fell to one knee, avoiding a blow that would have taken off his neck. Lunging, he wrapped Kren in a grapple, attempting to lift him from his feet. Kren's shield jammed into his shoulder, and the weight was too great. Unable to complete the tackle, Jerico shifted again, positioning his leg behind Kren's knee. The hilt of Kren's sword rammed down on the top of his head. Forcing through the pain, he shoved again, knocking the dark paladin to his back.

By now the crowd had reformed, and they were hurling insults and hissing at Kren. As Jerico pinned Kren's sword, he wished the crowd would do something useful, like tossing him a shield. He managed a few solid blows before Kren pulled his shield high enough to protect himself. The dark paladin struggled, unable to lift his sword with Jerico pinning his wrist, but armored as he was and his face now protected, Jerico knew he had little chance to do any more damage.

Unless ...

Hoping surprise would be on his side, he shifted so that his left knee pinned the blade. Fire burned into his flesh, and he screamed, but he did not relent. With both hands, he clutched Kren's shield, pulling it aside. Kren turned his head, expecting another blow, but that wasn't Jerico's plan. Instead he grabbed the inner handle, attempting to wrestle away control. Kren fought, but as Jerico gained further control, he saw a blessed sight: the light of his faith burning across the outer surface of the shield, peeling away the lion and turning the black paint to gold.

"I will break you!" Kren screamed. "You're a blasphemy! I will burn you with fire!"

Doing a good enough job already, Jerico thought, his entire left knee throbbing in unbearable pain. As the light swelled on his shield, Jerico lifted it higher, trying to press it against Kren's flesh. Before he could, Kren released the shield completely, and his fist smashed against Jerico's leg while filled with the fury of his god.

"Heretic!"

The dark energies swirled through his already wounded leg, bursting burnt flesh and shattering the bones of his knee. Jerico fell back, his mind white with pain. On pure instinct he clutched his shield before him, his only defense. Kren rose to his feet, blood dripping from his nose and one side of his face burned from where his cursed helmet had begun to melt from the proximity to the holy shield.

"My faith is stronger," Kren said, his upper body rising and falling with each labored breath. "Give Ashhur my contempt when I send you to him."

"Not today," Kaide said, having hidden amid the crowd. His dirk slipped through a gap near Kren's lower back, piercing his spine. Kaide's other arm wrapped about Kren's neck, holding him in place so he could not retaliate. After a moment, Kaide let him go. The paladin dropped, his eyes lifeless.

Seeing this, Jerico let go of the shield and collapsed. Kaide was over him in a moment, examining his knee.

"You ..." With the pain so great, Jerico struggled for every word. "You stabbed him in the back."

"I did," Kaide said, cutting off Jerico's pant leg so he could see the wound better.

"Not ... honorable."

Jerico laughed, delirious amid the pain.

"This world's life or death," Kaide said, frowning. "Like I give a damn about honor."

His vision fading, Jerico closed his eyes and tried to focus on his breathing. Around him, he heard murmured sounds of people talking.

"Carry him," someone said, most likely Kalgan. "Gently, please."

Hands grabbed him, and he screamed.

"I said *gently!* Watch for his leg. Gods, what a mess."

That was the last Jerico heard before he blacked out completely.

5

The numbers gathered for the offering stunned Darius. It seemed like the entire countryside had come to hear his words and receive Karak's blessing. Every time he glanced out from behind the curtain, he felt his chest tighten, and panic swell in his throat. The crowd waited in the courtyard, warmed by the thick clothes they wore and the few scattered fires built among them. Meanwhile, Darius remained in the castle, thinking of excuses for delay. When the service began, he would step out onto a balcony, and overlook the crowd from above as if he were their king.

"There's so many," Darius said, checking for what seemed like the tenth time.

"Of course," Sebastian said, adjusting his cloak. "Service is obligatory, or at least it was until our priest left, and we had no one to administer the offerings. Are you nervous, son?"

"Do not call me son," Darius said, harsher than he meant. "I am a warrior for Karak, and will not be insulted so."

"Of course, of course, I meant no offense. It's only a term of endearment for someone younger than I."

Darius looked to the curtain, and he listened to the impatient murmurings of the crowd. Seemed strange to him for service to be mandatory, but he'd heard of smaller towns having such rules, so it wasn't that unusual. Sometimes to cultivate faith, the faithless needed to be forced onto the path of righteousness.

"You're right," he said. "I am nervous. I've taught only in small villages. Out there ... how many, a thousand? Two?"

"Last census count? Four thousand and three hundred, at least within walking distance. Those too far away must give their tithes along with their taxes. But don't worry, Darius. I'll be at your side the whole time."

"You?" Darius asked.

"Why not?" Sebastian grinned at him. "It does good for the simple folk to see me beside you. It lets them know that we are their lords, the masters of their lives. To turn on one of us is to turn on the other. I will have no traitors to Karak in my household."

Darius struggled not to react.

"But what do you do when the priests of Ashhur come?"

The lord rolled his eyes.

"I say pretty words, toss them a few coins, and pretend to mull over having a second service for Ashhur. Their stays are not long. Lice-ridden beds and stale bread usually ensure that, though I'm not above a knife in the dark. I'm sure you understand."

Darius stood, and he pulled aside the curtain.

"I do," he said, stepping out onto the balcony. The crowd quieted, and they looked up to see a stranger. For a moment he said nothing, only scanned faces, judging reactions. Most were impatient, or bored. He saw plenty that clearly wanted nothing to do with giving offerings to Karak. Many still talked, not caring if they disturbed others. Forced faith, thought Darius. Was this its culmination? If he walked among them, he wondered if he'd find even a handful as faithful as his flock had been back in Durham.

"Welcome to the seventh day," Darius said. His voice failed him, and only the first few rows even knew he spoke. Battling his nerves, he swallowed, took another step toward the balcony's edge, and let his voice cry to the winds.

"Welcome to the seventh! Lift your voice, and let me hear your faith in our mighty god!"

The half-hearted murmurs nearly broke his heart. Only those near the front cried out, and they were so few. No, he thought. Perhaps their previous priest was a calm, quiet man. Faith in crowds was like a fire. Once it started to burn, it'd spread with incredible speed. He had to ignite it.

"In this day, we kneel to Karak and present our offerings for his protection, his strength, and his blessings. In this day, we of the faithful receive our reward for our loyalty. Are you faithful, people of the Yellow Rose?"

A bit more energy this time as they shouted yes. Darius smiled. He felt his nerves sliding away. This was no different than Durham. They needed to see his own faith, feel his own energy pouring out of him. And he would give it.

"I asked are you faithful?"

More shouts. They were waking up now, leaving their slumber to join the Lion.

"Then let us pray."

Darius drew his sword, flipped it about, and stabbed it into the balcony. Hands on his hilt, he bowed his head, but something was wrong. The crowd murmured, and immediately he knew he'd lost them. What was it? Opening his eyes, he realized his error.

His sword bore no flame. Even the common folk knew that its strength mirrored that of his faith.

"What is the meaning of this?" Sebastian asked, standing beside him with his hands clasped behind his back.

Darius opened his mouth to lie, then stopped. No, he would not profane his soul before thousands of witnesses.

"My faith in Karak is strong as ever," he said, just loud enough for Sebastian to hear. "But I fear I have displeased my god, and he has denied me his blessing."

Lord Hemman stepped away. A single motion of his hand sent guards rushing in, surrounding him. Down below the crowd erupted with confusion. Darius kept his sword where it was, though his grip on the hilt was strong enough to make his hands hurt. He eyed the guards, waiting for one to make their move.

"Do not make me cut you down while they watch," Sebastian said. "No matter if you deserve it or not. By Karak, how could I be so foolish? Now release your sword!"

Darius thought to resist, but he'd never make it out of the castle alive. More than ever, he felt revealed of his failure. Sebastian could give near exact count of the amount of men and women that had just seen the proof of Karak's displeasure with him. He would not go to the Abyss, not as he was.

"As you wish," he said, letting go of his sword and stepping away.

"Calmly," Sebastian said to his guards. They took Darius by the arm and led him away, and it wasn't until they were out of sight of the crowd that they clasped his hands behind his back and bound him. Darius repeated a litany of faith to Karak as Sebastian stepped back to the crowd, lifted his arms, and resumed the offerings as if nothing out of the ordinary had happened.

Hours later, Darius sat in the cold darkness, his hands chained to the wall. His arms ached from the uncomfortable position, but he refused to let it bother him. He would not give Sebastian the satisfaction. Even worse was the jailor. He lurked in the corner, barely visible in the smoldering light of a torch. Whenever Darius tried to move, or groaned with pain, the man would open his mouth to laugh, though he'd make no sound. Someone, perhaps even Sebastian, had removed his tongue. This jailor would tell no secrets, and make no bargains.

The door creaked, and then light pierced the darkness. Darius closed his eyes and prayed for the thousandth time to Karak for forgiveness.

"Well this is certainly interesting," Sebastian said. When Darius opened his eyes, he saw the lord standing at the entrance to his cell, torch in hand.

"Unnecessary is a better term," Darius said.

"Perhaps. I hope you know where you are. You're chained in the same cell Pallos was when you executed him in the name of Karak. I'm sure there's some irony here, though I won't know it yet until you tell me your story."

"I have no story to tell. I am a faithful servant of Karak."

"Then Karak has refused your service," Sebastian said, stepping closer to the bars. "Why is that, paladin? How did you fail?"

"I did not fail!"

Sebastian laughed as Darius blushed, ashamed of the outburst. What was happening to him, that he would lose his temper so easily?

"You humiliated me before my people," Sebastian said, pacing before the cell. His footfalls echoed with maddening consistency. "Some now claim the offerings are extra taxes clothed in the garb of faith. Others want your head, for they decry you an imposter. I've spread a few rumors of my own. My favorite is that you were pretending to be a paladin to make an assassination attempt on my life. So long as no one understands what's really going on, I can manipulate this to whatever outcome I desire."

"And what outcome is that?" Darius asked, feeling too tired for games. "What do you want with me? I did you no wrong. You heard my words. You know I speak truthfully of my faith in Karak."

"This isn't about you, boy," said Sebastian, and he grinned at Darius's reaction at the term. "This is about the rest of your kind. I've sent riders in search of the nearest priest or paladin of Karak that might know who you are, and what it is you've done to soil your name. What will they tell me when they return? What does the Stronghold think of the paladin named Darius?"

Darius closed his eyes and leaned his head against the cold stone.

"They'll say I am a murderer," he said. "They'll say I have turned against Karak and betrayed my Order."

"Did you?"

Eyes still closed, he shook his head.

"I don't know anymore."

Sebastian chuckled.

"Then I don't know, either. I won't pass judgment on you, just as I passed no judgment on Pallos. Your own kind will come for you, and do with you as they wish. Until then, you'll stay here."

"I'm sure the Stronghold will reward you well," Darius said as Sebastian turned to leave. "That's what really matters, I know."

The lord glanced back and smiled.

"Why, that thought never crossed my mind. Sleep well, Darius."

The door slammed shut, and the darkness returned once more. In that darkness, Karak's prophet laughed.

"Sleep now," Velixar said, waving an arm at the mute jailor. The burly man slumped in his chair and passed out. Stepping out from the shadows, the prophet crossed his arms and sighed. His red eyes, irises of fire, chilled Darius's blood and sent shivers up and down his spine.

"So this is where I find you, you who I thought held such promise? Locked in a dungeon, chained to a wall so you cannot even kneel in prayer to your god? Pathetic."

"What do you want?"

"Come now, don't act the idiot with me, even if you did seem somewhat dimwitted to Sebastian. You know what I want. I am no deceiver, no creature of lies. I told you my desire when we first met, and I'm not one prone to change."

Darius did everything he could to not meet that gaze.

"You want me to learn from you, to accept your word as the word of Karak. I still refuse, prophet."

Velixar laughed, and there was nothing pleasurable in the sound.

"Yes, because the world certainly agrees with you. Tell me, why am I the one with Karak's power, and you the fool locked in a cell? Why do the rest of the faithful refuse your wisdom? If even that egomaniacal Sebastian sees through your lies, what hope have you for the rest of Dezrel?"

"Always questions," Darius said. "How do I learn from you when you say nothing?"

Velixar walked over and brushed a pale finger across the jailor's forehead.

"I ask questions to show you have no answers, and will do so until you finally open your eyes and realize it."

The man in black shivered.

"Such wonderful dreams. This man has seen the dark side of this world, Darius, more than you could ever know. If anyone understands Dezrel's need for order, it is him."

"Will you help me escape?" Darius asked, feeling unclean as he did.

"Escape? No. Don't you see, this place, this moment, personifies you perfectly. Karak stands at the gate, ready to free you, and you simultaneously plead for aid while denying him his truths. You cannot have both, Darius. You cannot hold back Karak with one hand and reach for his help with the other."

Darius felt too tired, too lost to argue. He regretted even asking. Death at the hands of his brethren seemed better than going with the man with the ever-changing face. Still ... what if Velixar was right? What if he truly spoke the will of his god?

Velixar knelt before the gate, appearing to be in no hurry. The sun had set, and the jailor slept. They had all night.

"Do you know where you first erred?" Velixar asked.

Darius rolled his eyes. More questions. Always questions.

"I suppose you'll say when I refused to kill my friend?" he said, his voice full of sarcasm.

"No, that was just a symptom of a greater failure. It is when you treated him as your equal, as your friend. Call me a liar, and doubt my wisdom, but did you ever do the same to Jerico? You overlooked his lies. You forgave his belief in the false god. You treated him as one of your own, and in turn, spat in the face of Karak. Ashhur is the *enemy*. You cannot serve Karak and refuse that simple truth."

"No," Darius said, wishing he could call for the guards. "No. You're wrong. Karak doesn't want murder. He doesn't want bloodshed. He wants order! He wants peace!"

Velixar stood. All trace of humor left him. When he spoke, there was no mockery, no anger. Instead, Darius heard something all the more frightening: certainty.

"My eyes are everywhere," he said. "I watched you kill the paladin, Pallos. Answer me this one question truthfully, and I will let you be. What happened when you killed him? What happened when your blade cleaved through Pallos's neck?"

Darius fought against the memory. He had tried to think it made no sense, that it had been a hallucination, a delusion, a deception. The weight of it crushed him, and when he looked into Velixar's eyes, he knew he could not lie, so he said nothing, for what else could he say?

But Velixar knew. No smiles. No bragging. He spoke quietly, almost gently.

"Your blade burned with Karak's fire, didn't it? At that glorious moment, you felt the presence of your god."

Darius felt tears slide down his face.

"I did," he said, his voice cracking.

"You took the life of a paladin of Ashhur, and Karak blessed you for it. The truth could not be any simpler. Do you still deny me?"

He wanted to. He needed to. Shaking his head, Darius clung to the last vestige of his faith.

"Killing Jerico would have been wrong," he said. "You will never convince me otherwise."

Velixar put his back to him, and as the shadows swirled about, he spoke.

"I will not be the one to convince you, Darius. You will do that on your own. When you do, I will be waiting, and I will welcome you back to the glory of Karak with open arms."

The shadows thickened, and then Velixar was gone. Darius jolted, as if he'd been asleep the whole while. Tears remained on his face. In the corner, the jailor snored.

"Damn you, Jerico," Darius whispered. "I hope you live. I hope you live a thousand years for the suffering I must endure."

He slept, not long, and not comfortably. His dreams were dark, and Karak's contempt filled them with shadows and fire.

6

Kalgan sat beside him when Jerico came to, his consciousness swimming to the surface amid an ocean of pain.

"How long?" Jerico asked, lying very still, which kept the pain at its least.

"Just a few hours," Kalgan said. "You're tougher than you look."

"Thanks, I guess. Water?"

A bony hand pressed against his back as he sat up. Every movement made his leg ache, but he was thirsty, and refused to let the pain control him. He accepted a small wooden cup and drank. It tasted strangely bitter, but he downed it anyway.

"There's a few herbs in there to help you," Kalgan said, taking back the cup. "Some you've heard of, and some I doubt you've ever seen before. You'll sleep well, and it'll dull the pain. Ignore any strange hallucinations it gives you."

Already he felt his head turning light, and he tried to protest.

"I shouldn't ... things like that ..."

"Spare me, Jerico. Even in your sleep, you moaned with pain."

Jerico breathed in deep and tried to relax. Best he could tell, he was back in the same hut, and when he glanced left, he saw the patched up hole that had been his exit earlier. Beth was gone, and he hoped that meant her recovery was going well.

"Your ability to heal," Kalgan said, settling into his chair and resting his hands on his lap. "Can you use it on yourself?"

"In a way," Jerico said. His throat felt dry despite the drink, and his tongue thick. His pain was dulling, though, which was nice. "It requires concentration, and if the pain is bad ..."

"Which it is. I thought so. You won't be going anywhere for a few days. I suspect you'll be up and about faster than any man has right to, but it won't be today. I already told Kaide as much."

"Kaide?" Jerico started to sit up, but his stomach lurched, and the whole room swayed as if the world had begun to shake. He lay back down, deciding such complicated actions like sitting up or talking could probably be done slowly, or later.

"Yes, he seemed quite worried for you. Not that you'd get better, but that you'd run off. I told him you had a few days to recover, and I considered that generous. Most men would have never walked again, and those that did would use a cane. Your kneecap is in pieces, paladin. As for the flesh around it, well ... I wouldn't look if I were you. Not until you're ready to use Ashhur's magic to remedy it."

"Not ... magic ..."

Kalgan laughed, and Jerico chuckled along with him despite his sour mood.

"Call it what you want, but Kren did something to your leg when he touched you, that much I'm certain. I thought of cutting it off completely, to be honest. If I hadn't seen what you'd done for Beth, I'd have already brought out the knife."

"How is Beth?" Jerico asked after a moment to catch his breath. He felt a heaviness settling over him, like an invisible blanket weighted on all sides. He wanted to lie still, and do nothing, but he refused to cooperate.

"Still asleep, but in her own bed. Poor girl, to suffer such a cruel fate from a little thing like a spider. Some parts of life are lost to her, but she's resilient, got that much from her father. She'll find a way to thrive, and the people of this village love her. Don't worry about her fate, just concentrate on your own."

Ignoring Kalgan's earlier advice, Jerico sat up again. His eyes didn't want to open, but after a moment, he rubbed them with his fingers and then pulled aside his blanket. Seeing his leg, he turned to one side and vomited. Kalgan cursed up a storm.

"What'd I tell you?" Kalgan said. He left, then returned with a handful of dirt and sawdust to scatter atop the vomit.

"Does it smell of rot?" Jerico asked, pulling the blanket back over.

"No. For that, I guess you can be thankful."

Jerico laughed.

"Aye. Thankful. If you don't mind, I'm going back to sleep."

"Do you want me to splint the leg?"

Jerico thought of the black tissue around his swollen kneecap, the blue veins streaking outward in all directions.

"No," he said. "Don't touch it. Ashhur help me, I don't want to think of the pain."

Jerico slept, and when he awoke again, night had fallen. Several new blankets lay over him, and despite their cover, he felt cold all over. Kalgan's chair was empty beside him.

"Kalgan?" he asked anyway. His jaw trembled, but at least his head felt somewhat clear from whatever concoction of herbs the old man had given him. No one responded, and that was fine. He'd need silence for what would follow.

"Please be with me, Ashhur," he whispered as he shoved blanket after blanket aside. Shivers assaulted him, and he knew without a doubt he was with fever. No matter. He'd manage. Swallowing down his fear, he pulled away the last blanket, revealing his leg. This time he refused to look away from the swelling, bruises, and puss. His leg shook along with the rest of his body, and the movement awoke spikes of pain that nearly made him pass out. Gritting his teeth, he gently touched his knee with his fingertips.

Closing his eyes, he began his prayers to his deity. The broken bones would have to wait, for the curse of Karak was embedded in his flesh. If it'd been delivered to his chest or throat, he'd have been killed within an hour, if not instantly. At his leg, safely away from his lungs and heart, he'd survived, but it was only a matter of time. It was that curse he needed to banish. He tried to focus on it as he had done with Beth, but he felt drained, empty. Every shake of his fingers added to the pain, and his concentration repeatedly faltered. He wanted to lie down and sleep away the hours, but he knew it would only get more difficult with time.

"Please," Jerico whispered, panic starting to creep into his heart. "I don't know if I'm the last. I don't know what happened at the Citadel. But you can't have abandoned us. I just ... I can't believe that. Send me to my death if so, but otherwise, heal this damned leg of mine. I can't do it on my own. I can't."

Kren's words echoed in his head, strangely powerful.

My faith is stronger!

Perhaps so, but it wouldn't matter. He wouldn't let such a young whelp like him win. He wouldn't let him claim his leg, let alone his life, even if he had to demand the healing from Ashhur. Once more Jerico prayed, unable to hear his own words through the blood pounding in his ears. He prayed until he felt no pain, heard no sound, felt no chill.

Sleep took him.

Four days later, Jerico limped through the streets of Stonahm. Since healing Beth, he'd been treated the hero, and his belly was full of mulberry pie and sweet autumn cider. He wasn't completely sure it lacked any spirits, but he hoped Ashhur would be lenient.

"Good to see you about!" a man cried, and Jerico waved back politely, not having a clue as to his name. Slowly he headed toward the northern reaches of the town. The grass was much taller, and it felt uncomfortable brushing against his knee. He ignored it.

North of the town was a pond fed fresh water from a small stream, which often dried up completely until heavy rains came in the spring. The stream kept the water fairly clean, and the people of Stonahm cut the grass low about, swimming and bathing in its waters. Jerico found a log by the side and sat down, beyond relieved to take the weight off his leg. Waiting there for him was Beth, dressed in a pretty yellow dress.

"Thought you might not show," she said, smiling at him.

"Why's that?"

"Because you're old. Old people don't heal as fast as young people. That's what Kalgan says."

Jerico laughed.

"That so? Kalgan may be right, but you're wrong about me. I'm hardly old. See any grey hairs on my head?"

She rolled her eyes, obviously not impressed with his defense. Jerico laughed again, then quieted. His eyes fell on her left arm, which was hidden by a long sleeve that, while matching in color, was clearly a new addition. Reaching over, he carefully folded the sleeve twice, revealing the stump ending at the elbow.

"You shouldn't hide it," he said.

"Ma says ..." She blushed and looked away. "Ma says if I don't, the boys won't like talking to me, and no one will want to marry me."

He gently tucked a finger underneath her chin and forced her to look at him.

"Smile, and those boys will see nothing but how beautiful you are."

Her blush deepened.

"Are you ready for your exercises?" she asked.

Jerico took in a deep breath, then sighed.

"Yeah. Let's do it."

Beside the log was a simple creation Jerico had asked Kalgan to make for him. It was a heavy stone with a hole in its center. Through that hole Kalgan had threaded strong rope, forming a second loop along the top. It was that loop Jerico stuck his foot through, sliding it up to his ankle. Shifting his weight on the log until he was comfortable, he nodded to let Beth know he was ready.

"Any song in particular you'd like?" she asked.

"Sing your favorite. I'm sure I'll enjoy it."

The second day he'd been bedridden, though his skin had mostly healed, and only the bones needed to be knit back together. Beth had recovered from the bite, and come to him to express her thanks. While he lay there, still battling fever, she'd sung softly to him. Several times he'd drifted off to the sound of her voice, and awoken later to hear the same crystalline beauty. Because of her injury, she'd been excused from nearly all her chores, so when he'd begun preparing his recovery, she'd offered to help.

Beth sang a song of a highwayman in love with a forest maiden, and the whole while, Jerico struggled to lift the stone. He pretended the pain was an enemy, but if it truly was an enemy, it was defeating him. Kren's blow had eradicated much of his muscle, and while he'd tended it best he could, the newly healed flesh still felt withered, unreliable. Sweat dripped down his neck as he lifted again and again, sometimes pulling it an inch or two off the ground, sometimes not even budging it. Whenever he could, he focused on the lyrics instead of his pain. By the time Beth's song ended, he slumped, leaning back on his arms.

"Enough," he said. "I need a moment to breathe."

Beth nodded and said nothing. As he recovered, Jerico glanced at her, and finally decided to ask about something that had been bothering him.

"That boy, Ricky, he came to us in the forest when you were bitten. I thought I heard he was your brother, yet later Kaide said you were his only child left."

Jerico felt awkward asking, and was relieved when Beth rolled her eyes, clearly having had this conversation before.

"Ricky's not my real brother, nor is Ma ... Beverly my real mother."

Jerico nodded. He'd met Beverly, a plain but kind woman who was Ricky's mother. She'd come to thank him for what he'd done, once Kalgan had allowed people to visit.

"What happened to your mother?"

Beth brushed a strand of hair behind her ear.

"Do you want another song?" she asked.

Jerico nodded.

"Faster tempo, if you would."

This time she sang a ditty that'd be right at home in a tavern, and he forced the stone from the ground every single repetition. His knee burned, and the muscles of his lower leg quivered, but he did not relent.

When the fifth song was done, they called it quits. With Beth's help, Jerico limped down to the pond and splashed water across his face and neck, then dipped his leg below the cold surface. After another few minutes, he tried to stand on his own. He wobbled. Beth went to steady him, but he pushed her away.

"Should have taken Kalgan's offer up for a cane," he muttered. He'd made his way to the pond just fine, and by Ashhur, he was going to walk back to town as well.

"Maybe I should have sung shorter songs," she said as Jerico took another pained step.

"Then I would have made you sing more of them. I'm not daft, girl."

At her angry frown, he laughed.

"Sorry. You're right. Tomorrow, I won't push myself so hard. I promise."

"You said that yesterday, and you had to rest *three* times on the way back."

"I did, didn't I?"

"You did, and you broke your promise again today. Some paladin you are."

Jerico feigned a hurt look, and then he took another step, and feigning was no longer required. Step by step, they made their way back to the village. Jerico had every intention of collapsing back in his bed and sleeping for ten hours, but as they reached the edge of town, he heard a sound that made his stomach harden.

"What's going on?" Jerico asked, his voice low.

"Knights from Yellow Castle," Beth said. "Please, Jerico, go back. My father says ..."

He gently pushed her aside and turned the corner.

A man and a woman were there, the woman standing before the door to her home, which was shut behind her. Already parts of her dress were torn. The man towered over her, wearing chainmail and carrying a sword that swung from his hip, still sheathed. Her kissed her on the neck as she pleaded with him to stop.

"Tithes and taxes," the knight said. "You know you need to pay the lord his due."

When she turned away from him, he slapped her with his hand, which still wore a gauntlet. The metal bruised her face, and blood dripped from her swollen lip. Jerico took a step closer, unnoticed by either. Stunned, he looked about. They were not in hiding. At least three people walked past, and they kept their eyes ahead, refusing to even look. Anger swelled in Jerico's chest. He turned back around the corner, a fire in his eyes. Beth saw him and paled.

"Please, you can't interfere. You can't!"

"I can." He hobbled to a pen currently empty of animals, which were still out in the fields. Resting against one side was a shovel, and he took it. Its handle was long, sturdy. Maybe not as potent a weapon as his mace, but it'd do. Beth stepped back, chewing on her fingernails. Limping around the corner, Jerico thought he must look the most pathetic savior, but it didn't matter. He would not stand by and watch, no matter the reason, no matter what the rest of the village thought or did.

The woman's blouse was mostly torn, exposing one of her breasts. The knight had cast aside his gauntlets, one hand holding her wrist against the house, the other feeling wherever he wished. Jerico limped closer. The woman saw him, and her eyes widened. He swung. The flat side of the shovel connected with the back of the knight's head, which slammed forward, striking the door. His legs went weak, and he collapsed onto his rear. The woman stood shocked still, sobbing.

"Cover yourself," Jerico said to her. "And go to friends, or family. Now."

She pulled at her dress and rushed away, too scared to say a word. Jerico stood before the knight, holding the shovel in both hands. He kept his movements still, not wanting to reveal the weakness of his knee.

"You bastard," the knight said, spitting blood. "I'll gut you for that. This is Lord Sebastian's land, his town, and his fucking taxes."

"Were you looking for coins down her blouse?"

The knight grinned, revealing red-stained teeth.

"You really think you're gonna walk away from this? You're a farmer with a shovel."

He stood and drew his sword. His stance was uneven, his balance clearly shaken, no doubt from the blows to his head. Jerico shifted, planting his weight on his good leg.

"I used the flat side as a warning," Jerico said. "But this iron's heavy, and the sides are sharp. The next time I hit you, it will leave more than a bruise."

The knight's sneer showed how worried he was. Taking a step closer, he swung, a simple overhead chop. Jerico blocked it with the handle of his shovel, wielding it much as he would a staff. The wood was thick, and though the sword cut an indent, it was far from breaking through. Twisting the shovel, Jerico pushed away, changed its angle, and then struck him on the return swing. The metal end smacked into his exposed face, this time blasting free a tooth.

"I'm warning you," Jerico said. "That was still the flat side."

The knight collapsed against the side of the house, holding his free hand against his mouth. He said something, but it was muffled against his wrist. Jerico twirled the shovel, hiding the pain he felt. Even the act of swinging put horrible pressure on the joint. If the man managed to tackle him, bring him to the ground, Jerico would have little chance of wrestling free. He couldn't let him regain his confidence.

"What was that?" Jerico asked, keeping his outward image perfectly calm.

Instead of answering, the knight charged, no doubt hoping for surprise. Jerico had read him with ease, though. The knight had basic training, but was used to relying on his armor and sword to bully about simple farming people. Against someone like Jerico, his attacks were obvious, his strategies transparent. Flipping the shovel about, Jerico jammed the metal into the dirt, bracing it. The knight rammed himself against the other side of the handle, which slipped underneath the metal of his breastplate. The knight gasped, blood and spittle flying from his lips. The sword dropped from his hands, and then he rolled off to the ground.

His teeth clenched against the pain, Jerico walked without a limp to where the sword lay and took it. He tossed the shovel aside.

"Get up," Jerico said. "Walk out of this village, and go back to wherever you belong."

The knight rolled onto his knees and vomited. Jerico smacked his rear with the flat of his blade. Glaring, the knight staggered to his feet and headed south. Jerico watched him go, standing perfectly still until he was out of sight. When he was gone, he leaned all his weight on his good leg and let out a gasp.

"Jerico?" Beth asked, having stayed far away during the fight.

"Go find whoever that woman was," Jerico said. "Make sure she's all right."

"But ..."

"Go!"

She stepped back, her mouth open. The anger in his voice left her stunned. Turning, she ran. Jerico looked at the sword, glad to see no blood anywhere on its blade. By now, others had gathered around, whether from guilt, curiosity, or anger, he didn't know. But he knew how he felt. Seeing the people who had stood by and done nothing, he hurled the sword at them.

"Take it!" he shouted. "Let someone claim it as his own, and maybe next time, use it!"

He limped back to his hut, and on his way, not a soul dared meet his eye. Once there, he gathered what few things he had. Kalgan arrived not much later.

"You're leaving," he said, and it was not a question.

"I am."

"You're not healthy. We both know this. Where is it you'll go?"

Jerico sighed. "Back to the forest, with Kaide. I made a promise. I won't break it now."

"But the wildwoods are miles away, and on that leg ..."

"The walking will strengthen it as well as if I stayed here."

Jerico glared at him. He felt tired, exhausted, and drained. More than anything, he felt fury at the people there, whether it was fair or not. He would stay no longer. Jerico was no fool. He knew these things happened. But at least someone could have stepped in. Someone could have summoned a crowd, provided witnesses ...

"I'll prepare you some food," Kalgan said. He opened the door, but his hand remained against it, as if he were reluctant to leave. "What you did, it might put us in danger."

"Then I hope you deal with it better than you did that knight."

Stinging words, and he regretted them immediately. Kalgan looked at him with sad eyes.

"Fair enough," he said, shutting the door behind him before Jerico could apologize. He struck the wall with a fist, and once more wished the Citadel remained. If only he could return, be in the company and comfort of his brethren. They'd know what to do. They'd know what path was right.

Beth lingered outside when he stepped out.

"You'll need a guide," she said. "Kalgan says your horse is still here, and you can ride it back. Let me go with you."

He almost said yes.

"Does your Ma know you're here?"

Her guilty look was enough. Wanting no more reminders of Kren, the knight, or his injury, he took her by the shoulder and kissed her forehead.

"Stay here," he said. "And be strong."

Beth looked ready to cry, but she was made of sterner stuff than that.

"Goodbye, Jerico," she said, hurrying away.

Jerico found his horse and followed the road for several hours, letting the agony of his knee and the wind through his hair pull him away from that last pained look she'd given him, just before turning to run.

7

The story had spread like wildfire throughout the North, and the ears of the gray sisters were always attentive.

"It might be him," Claire had said the first time they heard it, sitting together in a crowded tavern at a cross-section of the main roads leading to the mountains.

"How could he be that stupid, though?" Valessa had asked. "Denouncing Karak to an entire crowd of gatherers? I don't believe it."

They'd headed for the Castle of the Yellow Rose just in case, for the drunk teller of the story had been adamant that the man remained there, imprisoned. On the way, they heard another telling, this one less embellished.

"A dark paladin with no flame," Valessa said. "We've found him."

"Perhaps Darius thought leading worship would restore his faith in the eyes of Karak," Claire said as they rode.

"It doesn't matter. No fire, no faith. Karak still wants him dead."

"Do we go in unknown, or demand an audience with Sebastian?"

Valessa bit her lip.

"He's in custody, and his punishment ours. We go, and reveal our nature to their lord. It'll be his head if he tries to deny us our rightful prisoner."

It'd been three days since the event, if the stories were to be believed. The wind was cold, the road hard and rocky, as they rode toward the castle. At the gates, two guards stopped them, demanding names and reasons for their visit.

"I'm Claire, and this is my sister Valessa," Claire said, going with their standard cover. "As for our occupation, let's just say you soldiers would greatly prefer ..."

"No," Valessa said, interrupting her. She leapt off the back of their horse, not worried that the guards drew their weapons. She threw back her hood and stood at her full height.

"I am Valessa, sister and servant of Karak, come from Mordeina to speak with your lord, Sebastian Hemman. Let us through, and escort us if you must. Our business is urgent, and we will not discuss it here."

"Have you any proof of this?" asked one of the guards, seeming less impressed than the others.

"Proof?" Valessa asked, smiling at him.

"Valessa ..." Claire warned, still astride her horse.

Valessa ignored her, and instead approached the doubting guard. Slipping her hand down her shirt, she pulled out a pendant from beneath her armor. It was the face of a lion, its mouth open, its teeth bared.

"You wonder if I serve Karak?" she asked. "If I am his powerful servant? Listen closely, dimwitted man, and I will speak to you your proof."

Her gaze held him. There was a charm in her words, and power in her eyes. The others watched as she slipped beside him, ran a finger along his neck, and then brushed his ear with her lips. She took in a soft breath, and then unleashed the fury of Karak. It was not her voice that screamed, but that of the Lion. The others clenched their hands against their heads, but the guard stood still, his mouth open. Blood dripped down his neck, spilling from his ears. When the roar ended, he collapsed.

"He'll live," Valessa said as the others lifted their swords. "Though he'll never hear from that ear again. Would anyone else like proof?"

They let the gray sisters through, along with an escort of six nervous soldiers. Inside the castle, they waited several minutes, until at last a knight came forward and gestured for them to follow. They came before Lord Sebastian Hemman sitting on his throne, soldiers at either side of him. Valessa snickered at the protection. So cute.

"Greetings, ladies of Karak," Sebastian said, rising. "Consider me honored to have such revered guests come to my home. I hope the guards at the gate did not trouble you."

"No trouble," Valessa said, and Claire turned her head to hide her smile.

"I must confess, I'm not familiar with your Order. Are you paladins, or perhaps priestesses?"

"We are what we are, and that is none of your concern," Claire said, her humor vanishing. "Know only that we speak for the Stronghold, and for Karak. Word has come to us of a prisoner, and we believe him one we have hunted for the past weeks."

"Leave me," Sebastian said to his soldiers, holding up a hand for the two women to pause. The soldiers began filing out, and none looked too happy with leaving their lord alone.

"No, Gregane," he said, stopping one of the knights. "You stay."

The burly knight stepped back, staying at the right hand of his lord.

"The man you seek," Sebastian said when the rest were gone. "Would you care to tell me his name?"

The gray sisters exchanged a look, and Claire shrugged.

"Darius," Valessa said. "His name is Darius, and he once hailed from the Stronghold."

Sebastian stroked the hairs of his chin as he leaned back in his seat.

"Have you come to find him," he asked, "or kill him?"

"Does it matter?" Claire asked.

"It does, for you see, I had a very strange visitor last night. His words of caution are ... difficult to shake."

Valessa felt her stomach tighten, and she did not miss Claire's eyes narrowing in anger.

"This visitor," Valessa asked, "was he a man with many faces, and eyes that burned like fire?"

Sebastian looked surprised, but he hid it well.

"He was. And he told me that while orders were initially given to execute Darius, circumstances have changed. He said I'd soon receive new orders from the Stronghold, signed by the hand of the High Enforcer."

"Let me guess," Claire interrupted. "Those new orders would hand Darius over to him, the prophet?"

Sebastian shrugged. "Something to that effect."

Valessa bit down a curse. She turned to Claire and lowered her voice to a whisper.

"The commoners must never know of conflict between servants of Karak," she whispered. "Do we dare challenge Velixar's authority?"

"Sebastian is no commoner. Surely a lord understands that even servants must sometimes quarrel."

"My ladies, if I may interrupt." Sebastian smiled at them, and something opportunistic glinted in his eyes that made Valessa wary.

"What is it?" Claire asked, no pretense of politeness in her words.

"Now, for all I know, last night was just a strange dream, and gods are known to work in mysterious ways. Ashhur may have come in the guise of his enemy to save the life of a traitor, for example. To be prudent, I will wait some time for new orders, but until then, I know of another who is an enemy of Karak, whose death I think would benefit us all."

Valessa felt her anger grow, at both the lord and the prophet.

"We are not assassins to be directed as you wish," Claire seethed.

"I understand. I am simply suggesting a wise use of your time while I wait for new orders. Now, should you perform this duty, and return without me having heard word from the Stronghold ..."

He let his voice trail off as he took a drink of wine. The sisters exchanged another glance. Valessa could tell Claire wasn't happy about this, but short of executing Sebastian, there weren't too many options currently available to them.

"I knew we should have come unnoticed," Claire whispered.

"Who is your target, the one that is such an affront to Karak?" Valessa asked.

Sebastian downed the rest of the glass, licked his lips, and set it aside.

"My older brother, Arthur. He lives in his castle, quite the recluse. But those of his retinue spread word of how the worship of Karak in our lands is unlawful, our enforcements unfair, and the tithes the people pay unjust. His castle is small, but well-guarded, and could withstand a siege for at least a year. The Castle of Caves, they call it. But you two ladies ..."

"I know where the castle is," Claire said. "Now give us your word that when we return, Darius will be ours to deal with as we desire."

"If no orders have been delivered to me stating otherwise."

Claire's smile was rigid as stone.

"Of course."

"Wait," Valessa said before they could be excused. "I wish to see Darius first, with my own eyes."

Sebastian frowned. "Lady, I can assure you that he is in our custody, and properly taken care of."

She shook her head.

"My own eyes, Sebastian. That is my demand, and I will not relent."

The lord glanced at Gregane, who nodded.

"Very well," Sebastian said, standing. "Follow me, but you must come alone. Gregane will have his eye on you at all times. No tricks. Any attempt made on Darius's life will be treated as an attempt on my own."

Both of which you could never stop, Valessa thought, but instead she smiled and followed him past his throne and into the dungeon below. It was dark, damp, and smelled of blood and piss. She caught the jailor hiding in the corner, as if frightened to be seen in the presence of his lord. Valessa gave him little thought, for her attention was reserved for the man chained to the wall.

"Darius?" she asked, approaching the bars.

"Careful," Gregane said, his sword drawn. "He is a dangerous man, after all."

Valessa knew that wasn't why he kept his blade at ready, but pretended otherwise. She tilted her head, waiting for her eyes to adjust to the dim light. The bound man didn't seem like a paladin of Karak. He looked pale, tired, with his eyes sunken into his face. He was half-naked, wearing only torn underclothes. In the light of day he might have been handsome, but down there, he looked deserving of only pity.

But she had no pity for a betrayer.

"My, my," Darius said, laughing. "They sent a gray sister after me? Am I that great a threat to Karak, that I must die in secret?"

"You revealed your lack of faith before a crowd of thousands," Valessa said. "While in full armor no less, still bearing the crest of the Lion. For that alone you should die."

"Perhaps. I thought killing Nevek and Lars was the greater crime, but what do I know?"

"There, you have seen him," Sebastian said, clearly impatient. "May we return to more pleasing environs?"

"Are you not here to kill me?" Darius asked. He laughed again. "Such a shame. What happened, sister? Have you lost your courage?"

Her hand reached for the dagger at her side, but Gregane was there, holding her wrist.

"I wouldn't do that," he said.

Valessa glared, debating. She was in the dungeon of a castle, with a hundred soldiers waiting on call. Was it really worth dying over a pathetic, failed paladin?

"Forgive me," she said, pulling her arm free of his grasp. "I have little patience when in the presence of heretics."

"Heretic?" For the first time, Darius spoke in anger. "*Heretic?* What heresy have I committed? What blasphemy have I spoken against Karak? I worship him still, with all my heart. Consider me lost, gray sister, and consider me a failure, but do not dare presume to understand the nature of my faith."

Valessa didn't know what to say, so she stated the most obvious argument against him.

"Then why does Karak not bless you? Why does he deny fire to your blade?"

She stepped closer, and Gregane followed. The light of his torch bathed over Darius, and for the first time she saw his blackened hand and gasped.

"You bear the mark," she said, her voice nearly a whisper.

"I know."

"The black hand ... that is not given lightly. Save your lies. Nothing you say can disprove the truth of Karak burned into your flesh."

Darius fell silent, and she waited for an answer. He offered none. Turning, she glared at Sebastian.

"You play dangerous games," she said, "daring to interfere with the will of Karak. I'll do as you ask, this one time, only because even in Mordeina we hear of your reputation as a faithful servant. But do not test me, and do not dare betray me."

"Is that a threat?" Gregane asked, but Sebastian only smiled.

"Of course, milady," he said. "Now let us return to the light."

When they reentered the throne room, a knight stood beside Claire, looking angry and impatient.

"Lord Hemman, if I could have a word," he said, but Sebastian cut him off.

"Show respect, Sir Mark. I have guests not yet dismissed. Speak out of turn again, and I will have your tongue."

The knight looked flustered but obeyed.

"Would you like to stay here for the night?" Sebastian asked as Valessa joined Claire's side.

"We should begin our ride," Claire said. "The Castle of Caves will take us time to reach, even on horseback. Until we meet again."

Neither bowed as they left.

"Is Darius there and alive?" Claire asked as they exited the outer gate.

"He is."

"Did you speak with him?"

"I did. He bears the mark of the abandoned, Claire. It covers his entire hand. Never have I seen one so hated by Karak."

Claire nodded.

"Then it will be good to get this business done, and execute such a faithless traitor."

Valessa frowned at the word faithless. So strange. She heard the desperate faith in Darius's voice. No one was as skilled a liar as that, to put on such a performance. She didn't want to imagine the turmoil that must be within his soul.

"The sooner, the better," Valessa agreed, wishing to think no more on the matter.

"The women are dangerous," Gregane said when the gray sisters were gone. "Perhaps it would have been better to hand over the paladin now."

"Even the faithful are willing to make deals to reach their ends," Sebastian said, waving dismissively. "I captured Darius, not them, and I will consider this my reward. Arthur's been a thorn in my side long enough."

He glanced over to where Sir Mark waited, hands behind his back and his head bowed.

"What is it?" he asked, annoyed.

"The people of Stonahm," the knight began. "They've rebelled against your rule."

Sebastian poured himself a cup of wine and sipped it. He felt his veins turn to ice as the words sank in.

"How so?" he asked at last.

"I'd come for tithes, but instead of handing them over, one of their men assaulted me when my back was turned. I was beaten, and sent away with orders never to return."

"You were there for tithes, and just tithes, I assume?"

"Of course, milord."

Sebastian hurled the glass, which shattered against the knight's breastplate. The wine splashed across the armor, staining it purple.

"Do not treat me like an idiot, Mark. You mistook tits for tithes again, didn't you? Get out of my sight."

Sir Mark flushed and, still dripping, turned and exited the room. Sebastian sat back in his chair and snapped his fingers. A servant lurking behind a curtain heard, and he quickly came with another glass.

"What must be done?" Gregane asked.

"I have Arthur harassing me from his castle, Kaide from the forest. One I can't get to, and the other I can't find. This will not go on. If the peasants think, for even a moment, they can get away with challenging my authority, a full-blown revolt will not be far behind."

"Give me a hundred men," Gregane said. "I will teach them a lesson the whole North will talk about."

Sebastian accepted the cup from the servant, and filled it with more wine.

"To Stonahm," he said before downing it. "Go put fear into the heart of the North."

8

Jerico had wondered how he'd find his way back to Kaide's hideout, but his worries were unfounded. Reaching the forest was easy enough, the path simple and often traveled. At the edge of the trees, he set up camp and slept, making sure his fire burned long and with plenty of smoke. When he awoke the next morning, his horse was gone.

"Huh?" he grunted, realizing the absence. He hadn't been alerted by Ashhur to any danger, so he assumed it was members of Kaide's band. His supplies lay beside him, and he prepared his morning meal while the few remaining birds sang in the bare treetops. After awhile, he sensed eyes watching him, and he grinned.

"You've taken my horse," he called out. "The least you could have done was take me with him."

A pause, and then the bandit stepped out from hiding. He was hardly the thief he expected.

"Ricky?" Jerico asked.

The boy nodded. He stood erect, as if willing himself to appear taller, more mature.

"I had to make sure you was you," he said.

"Well, I am I," Jerico said. "Care to lead me back to camp?"

Ricky gestured, and Jerico slung his pack across a shoulder and followed.

"No one thought you was coming back," Ricky said. "But they left me here just in case you did. They're all killing soldiers, so no one could stay and watch."

"Killing soldiers?" Jerico asked, ducking underneath a low branch. They followed no path, just pushed through the brush and leaves deeper and deeper into the woods.

"Don't think you can get me to talk," he said. "I'm smarter than that."

"Of course, I certainly don't mean to offend." Jerico gave him a moment to cool off, then continued. "Beth's fine, by the way. I don't know if anyone told you."

"Kaide told me."

Ricky shot a glance behind him, and for a moment he looked like the young, indecisive kid he was.

"Thank you," he said.

"Did it for her, not you, but you're welcome anyway."

The camp was silent as they entered, empty as Ricky had said.

"Where are they?" Jerico asked. "If they're fighting, perhaps I can help."

Ricky grew flustered.

"Too far to walk, and you couldn't even if you wanted to."

The door to one of the cabins opened, and it turned out the camp wasn't completely empty.

"Our hero returns," Sandra said, and she laughed at Jerico's over-exaggerated bow.

"I could never stay away from you for long," he said, shooting her a wink. Ricky rolled his eyes, then yawned long and loud. Jerico remembered the boy had stolen his horse during the night, as well as how far the walk had been from there to the forest's edge.

"Have you been up all night?" he asked.

"Kaide says sometimes men have to go days without sleep."

"And sometimes men go days without food or water, but it doesn't help them none. Go to sleep, Ricky. I didn't come all this way just to run off again. Besides, Sandra's here. She'll stab me if I try anything."

Ricky relented, casting one last watchful eye on the two of them before vanishing into his cabin.

"I'm not sure I feel safe around you alone," Sandra said.

Jerico opened the door to his own little hut and tossed his supplies inside.

"Don't worry too much. With this limp, I doubt I could catch a crone."

"Catch me? I wouldn't run, paladin. I'd knock you flat and crush your testicles for the attempt. And you don't want to imagine what Kaide would do afterward."

"Would he make me tonight's supper?"

Sandra laughed, but the laugh died when he limped toward the stable.

"Your leg," she said. "Does it hurt much?"

Jerico shrugged.

"It's bearable," he said. "I'll pray over it soon, like I should have this morning. Much of the pain is just weakened muscle, and lingering effects of a curse."

At the stables, he found his horse tied and fed, and the saddle properly removed. Patting the horse's side, he took a breath and steadied himself. His knee throbbed, the rough travel through the forest feeling like it'd removed every bit of progress he'd made the past few days. He put on a tough show, though, and tried to minimize the limp as he walked back to the center of the hideout. He made it halfway there before he leaned against a home and groaned, tilting his head back with his eyes closed.

"Let me see the leg," Sandra said, her playful tone gone. Sighing, Jerico rolled up his pant leg, and even he winced at the sight. A purple bruise covered the entire knee. The bones were healed, though the surface of his kneecap was oddly shaped, as if it hadn't smoothed out upon rejoining. The surrounding skin was swollen red, and when she pressed her fingers against it, he let out a gasp.

"Damn fool," Sandra said. "You walked all the way through the forest on that?"

"It felt better at the time."

"Get to your bed, or beside the fire if you'd like. I need to start it soon, anyway. When Kaide and his men return, they'll be eager for a feast to celebrate their victory."

"And if they lose?" Jerico asked as he accepted her help, leaning half his weight upon her.

"Then they'll need food and drink to toast the memory of the fallen. Either way, we'll need meat."

The two hobbled to his cabin, and she laid him down on the bed. The relief was immediate.

"Join me when you wish," Sandra said, shutting the door behind her as she left.

Finally alone, Jerico spent time in prayer, pouring healing magic into his knee. He knew he should have stayed in Stonahm. He was traveling on a leg mere days after an injury most would take months to recover from. But the way the people of the village had looked at him, as if he had been in the wrong protecting that woman ... he didn't want to feel those eyes upon him anymore. As he prayed, the pain subsided, and the swelling lessened. He sighed with relief. Didn't look like he'd added any permanent damage.

When finished, he ate the last rations from his pack, then stepped outside. The air had a bite to it, and the burgeoning fire Sandra built called out to him. Grabbing a blanket off the bed, he laid it down beside the bonfire.

"I'll keep quiet so I don't wake you," Sandra said as she tossed on another log.

"Much appreciated."

The crackling of the fire soothed him, and he was halfway asleep when he heard Sandra say his name.

"Jerico ... thank you for saving my niece."

"Welcome," he said, eyes still closed. He felt her lingering nearby, though, so he opened an eyelid and looked over. She was staring at his leg, still exposed since he had not rolled down the pant leg after his prayers.

"The man, Kren ... why did he attack you?"

Jerico let his head drop back to the dirt.

"Kaide told you about that, I take it? Guess there's no reason to hide it. He attacked me because I might be all that's left. Karak's paladins have begun a secret war, one I fear we've already lost. My brothers, my home ..."

His voice trailed off, and he listened to the fire burn.

"Don't you hate them for it?" Sandra asked.

"I shouldn't. Ashhur forgive me, I often do, but I shouldn't. I can't hate, Sandra. It'll destroy everything I am. Maybe that makes me a fool. Maybe that's why the world will soon move on without me. But I won't hate them. Pity, yes. Remorse. Sadness. I'll even kill if I must, and bloody my hands to protect the life of another. But I won't hate."

It took her a long while before Sandra could respond.

"After everything that's happened, I fear my brother knows only hatred."

"Then I'll pray for him, if you'd like."

"Please do."

Her footsteps trailed off as she left the fire unattended. Jerico prayed for them both, as he'd promised, and then did his best to forget it all so he might sleep.

The sound of arguing woke him sometime later. Jerico sat up, his hand reaching for the weapon he no longer had.

Shaking dirt and leaves from his hair, he glanced at the sky to gauge the time. Late afternoon. His knee felt stiff, but the pain had lessened. Standing with his weight on the other leg, he waited for the men to arrive. Sandra joined him not long after, carrying a slab of salted meat.

"They're angry," she said, her voice low. "Do you think ..."

"Assume nothing," Jerico said, helping her set up the spit. "Only hope for the best, and pray against the worst."

Despite his words, Jerico also thought a rough defeat had befallen them, but it seemed that was not the case. When the first of many men appeared, they lacked a single wound upon their bodies.

"It doesn't matter that I couldn't have killed them all," Bellok grumbled as he and Kaide walked toward the bonfire. "Packed together and unaware, I would I have wiped out half of Sebastian's men before they even knew ..."

"Jerico," Kaide said, seeing the paladin. He approached with his back to Bellok, who clearly did not appreciate the interruption.

The rest of the men were joining them, all grumbling amongst themselves. Most ignored him, though a few, the Irons twins in particular, did their best to greet him warmly.

"I took too long building the fire," Sandra said. "I'm sorry. I've just begun."

"And what you've got won't be enough," Kaide said. "Adam, go grab us something more to eat. I think all of us could use a bit of blood in our bellies."

"Be better if we had blood on our blades instead," Adam muttered as he headed off to one of the buildings.

"Such dour moods," Jerico said. "What is so terrible?"

"We had our ambush prepared," Bellok said, sitting on a heavy log beside Jerico. "We expected only a handful of knights, but instead a good forty marched toward us. With my magic alone, I could have—"

"You could have cooked one inside his armor, maybe two," Kaide said, drawing his dirk and stabbing it into the log he sat on. "We were outnumbered, and they were armed and mounted. We'd have been slaughtered."

"We had surprise," one of the men muttered.

"They can't stand toe to toe with us!" Griff hollered, and the rest of the men echoed approval.

"Is that what you want?" Kaide asked. "To have charged out of the forest and died, just to kill a few random knights? Which of you, in your plain clothes and leather boots, would have withstood a single blow from their swords? Which of you has the strength to crack a chestplate of iron with only a wooden club?"

The men fell silent, until Adam reappeared, holding a slab of meat.

"I coulda," he said.

Kaide looked up at him, and for the first time since returning, he smiled.

"I don't doubt that, Adam. All of you, I don't doubt you. But I don't want to lose you, no matter what. The advantage wasn't ours. One day, it will be, and we'll break their necks and send their horses running to the four corners of Dezrel."

"Bet if Jerico was with us ..."

Jerico didn't catch who said it, but Kaide did.

"You got something to say, Barry?"

Of the many men gathered, the shortest of the lot stepped forward, a thin man with a long beard. When he spoke, Jerico recognized him as the amusingly cranky jailor from before.

"Yeah, I do. I bet if Jerico was with us, you'd have given the order. You wish we all was him, don't you? Wish we had training, fancy armor, and weapons that cost more than everything we ever owned put together. It's been three years, Kaide. When's the time gonna be right? When we ever gonna make them pay for what they did to us at Ashvale?"

The crowd fell silent, and the chill in the air was colder than it'd been all night, paying no heed to the fire. Jerico glanced between them, wondering if he'd need to intervene. His place or not, he wouldn't watch one of them murder the other.

"Of course I wish I had knights," Kaide said, his voice deathly quiet. "Of course I wish for weapons, armor, and horses. I wish Lord Hemman was dead, and I could piss on his corpse while the whole world watched. But that don't matter none. I'd trade every single one of those wishes to have Lisbeth in my arms one more night. You got a problem with how I lead, then you go right ahead and leave."

In the following silence, Sandra's soft voice carried the power of a thunderclap.

"None of you are here because of my brother. You're here because of Sebastian, because of what he did. I haven't forgotten. Have you, Barry? Have you forgotten the smiling face of your little Mary?"

Barry stepped back, as if ashamed.

"I'm sorry, Kaide. You too, Sandra. I do miss my girl, but I got boys and a wife at Stonahm. They been waiting three years for me to come home. What we done all this time? We've hurt Sebastian, cost him some coin, but we're no closer to taking back our home. We're no closer to victory. This ain't a war we can win. It's not even a war. We're a fly buzzing 'round the ears of a horse, just biting."

Barry left for his room. Jerico watched him go, while the rest of the men looked the other away. Kaide muttered a curse under his breath. Conversation took awhile to restart, but when it did, it was on a hundred other things than the failed ambush that night. The smell of cooking meat wafted over them, and Jerico felt his own stomach growl.

"What is it you're cooking?" Jerico asked Adam, who was turning the spit.

"Leftover knight," Adam said, grinning.

"Enough," Kaide said. "I'm tired of that damn joke. It was never funny."

The bandit leader stood and left. When it seemed no one would follow, Jerico looked to Sandra.

"Go," she said. "I know him. He'll want to talk, but only to someone he trusts will listen."

Jerico stood and limped after.

"I prefer to be alone with my thoughts," Kaide said as Jerico approached. He leaned against a heavy pine outside the ring of their homes, his back to the fire.

"We paladins are known for being intrusive."

"That you are."

No humor in his voice, just barbs. Jerico shrugged it off.

"You wanted my help once. You still do?"

Kaide glanced at him with red-veined eyes.

"Do I? Of course. But you heard the men. What does it matter? We're just flies."

Jerico crossed his arms and leaned against another pine, relieved to remove some weight from his knee. He watched Kaide for a while, saying nothing. He always considered himself a good judge of character. Many times he'd encountered outlaws, and they had a vibe about them that Kaide lacked. None of the rest seemed quite right with it, either. This wasn't a ploy for coin. This wasn't a man taking something because he could, or because he thumbed his nose at authority. Something more was at stake. Ashvale ... What had happened at Ashvale?

"I want to help you," Jerico said. "But I have to believe I'm doing the right thing. Tell me why you do this. Tell me the reason you fight. Who were you before this started?"

"Who was I?" Kaide laughed, and he looked to the darkening sky. "I was Kaide Goldflint, son and heir to a fortune, a fortune stolen away from me by Lord Sebastian Hemman. Will that suffice?"

Jerico shook his head.

"No, it won't. What happened there? Three years ago, Barry said. Help me understand."

Kaide rubbed his eyes with his fingers.

"Sebastian controlled much of the North, but he'd never laid claim to the rough lands nestled against the Elethan mountains. A few of us, my father in particular, spent years scouting the land, setting up exploratory mines, searching for veins. When we found them, we kept it secret, and acted fast. My father set up a guild, uniting several towns together. Sebastian was furious, but our lands were our own, and our mining guild spent enough bribes in Mordeina to keep the king from siding against us. We endured heavy taxes, taxes you couldn't imagine, but we still had our land, our homes, and our wealth.

"Three years ago, that ended. That coward didn't even send in his knights, for he feared King Baedan's punishment. So instead, he rounded up thousands of homeless and poor in Mordeina and gave them deeds to our land. He convinced them they were legit, told them of our wealth, and sent them on their way. You can't imagine the bloodshed that followed. We tried to make peace with the first few, giving them jobs or minor parcels of land. But they kept coming. They'd spent all they had believing Sebastian's lie. Left with nothing, they would rather die ..."

Kaide sighed.

"And die they did. Still, it wasn't enough. So come winter, Sebastian finally sent in his knights. They didn't kill a soul, only came for more 'taxes'. Every bit of food, they took. They slaughtered our animals. They burned our storehouses. The winter was harsh, and he came after the first snow. By the time we could get a messenger to Mordeina, the King had already been convinced by Sebastian that bandits were running amok because our lands were lawless, ungoverned. We received no aid. And without food, and no game to hunt ..."

Jerico put a hand on Kaide's shoulder as the man closed his eyes and looked away to hide his tears.

"We starved. My mother and father, they were too old ... I lost a brother. My wife. Every one of these men here, they lost children, family, or friends. And what we had to do to survive ... am I cursed man, Jerico? Am I doomed in death for what I did, to survive, to keep my sister and little girl fed?"

"The stories," Jerico said, his voice almost a whisper.

"Kaide the cannibal," the bandit leader said, laughing darkly. "Come spring, we were too weak to fight back. More crowds filled the roads north, carrying deeds, and this time Sebastian came with the King's authority to enforce them. Every last man, woman, and child of Ashvale was sent south, to make a living elsewhere."

"You founded Stonahm," Jerico said, piecing it together.

"I don't want Sebastian to know where we live," Kaide said, nodding. "I don't want him to strike those we love. That's why they're so far away. We have all said goodbye to our wives and families, seeing them only when it is safe. This we endure to make Sebastian pay. It may seem we have no chance, but I have one last secret, one I cannot tell even you. Not yet. Some of the men don't even know. But if we can stir up enough anger, kill enough knights, I know we can retake our home ..."

Jerico closed his eyes and thought over the words. With Ashhur's gift, he could sense anytime a man lied, and he'd not once felt that betrayal. Every word was truth. They'd been systematically assaulted, starved, and removed from their lawful home. If there was ever a rightful cause, it was Kaide's.

"What do you mean, retake your home?" Jerico asked, suddenly realizing the true meaning of the words.

"Those people currently in Ashvale are thieves and robbers," Kaide insisted. "I've watched the roads, and we've intercepted every shipment of food possible. Same for the gold they send south to Lord Sebastian. One day we'll have enough strength, enough people, to march north and take our lands back."

Jerico shook his head.

"I'll help you, train your men and lead them into battle, but only against Sebastian's knights. I won't help you murder the people who took your homes. They thought they were the lawful owners, Kaide. The law told them they were right, and both lords and kings agreed."

"You'd have me forgive them?"

"I'd have you let it go. You're an honorable man. You've already sworn your life to vengeance. Must you yearn to repeat the bloodshed done against you?"

Kaide shook his head.

"You can't understand. You weren't there, watching helplessly as your loved ones withered and starved. You don't fall asleep to red dreams filled with such hatred even Karak would be put to shame. But I'll accept your help, and gratefully. Tomorrow morning, begin the training. I have a few weapons we stole from the knights, but truth be told, I haven't given most out yet for fear no one knows how to use them. With you, I can make sure they don't put the pointy end in themselves. We're in the right on this, Jerico. Outlaw or not, Sebastian needs to suffer."

"Outlaw," Jerico said, and he chuckled. "Is there such a thing as an outlaw paladin? Sounds like a contradiction."

"Hardly," Kaide said, smacking him across the shoulder. "I have a feeling every true paladin is already an outlaw in this world."

Kaide led him back to the fire, where the rest of the men were busy eating.

"Starting tomorrow, he'll be your trainer," he shouted to them. "And come our next ambush, he'll be right there with us, standing against our foes."

"Does this mean I get my armor and mace back?" Jerico asked as the men cheered half-heartedly. Kaide laughed, his good humor finally returning.

"All yours. You won't regret this, Jerico. Not at all."

Jerico prayed he was right.

9

In the darkness, Darius called out for the prophet.

"I am here," Velixar said, stepping out from the shadows and into the light of the single torch. Beside him, the jailor slept, and with a touch, Velixar made sure he stayed that way.

Darius hung his head. He couldn't even look at the man in black when he spoke. But he saw no other way. He had to find out. Denying Velixar without proof, without certainty, only risked him remaining a fool.

"One chance," he said. His dry throat cracked his voice. "I'll give you one chance, but that is all. I will listen, and see if Karak's truth is with you."

"Do you tire of this cell?" Velixar asked, approaching the bars. "Do you tire of your chains?"

Even swallowing hurt. It'd been a day since he'd had a drink, and he felt so tired, so thirsty. His back throbbed with every beat of his heart. His arms felt like torn, twisted limbs, never to regain their natural shape.

"Yes. I do."

Velixar smiled.

"If only you could feel the cage about your soul as keenly as you feel those chains. Be free, Darius."

A wave of his hand and the door opened. Another, and his bindings became like shadow, his flesh falling right through them. Darius's back popped as he twisted left and right, gasping in pain as his muscles fired off random spasms. Despite the pain, it felt deliriously good to stand. He took an unsteady step toward Velixar, then another. The prophet held out his hand, and Darius took it. There was no warmth to the grip.

"Sustenance first," Velixar said, his ever-changing face smiling. "Then learning."

The torch flickered and died, and in the dark, they walked forward. Darius felt a momentary sickness, and then he was beneath open stars. He shivered at the cold. They stood on a tall hill, and when he glanced back, he saw the Castle of the Yellow Rose.

"Wait here," Velixar said. "I must gather your things the guards took from you."

Another portal of shadow ripped open before him, and then he stepped through, leaving Darius alone.

"Is this your will?" Darius whispered as he shivered. "Is this what you want, Karak? My god, please, show me your way. I'm tired of being lost."

He looked to his blackened hand, and he wondered if the mark would ever be gone. Several minutes later, Velixar returned, tossing down a chest. It must have weighed a ton, and it thunked heavily against the grass, but the prophet showed no strain at all.

"Nearby is a stream," he said. "The cold will not harm you, though it will be unpleasant. Consider it symbolic. Once you've cleansed yourself, come back and put on your armor. I would see the man you once were standing before me."

Darius stumbled in the direction Velixar pointed, and sure enough he found a small stream winding its way south through the hills. He caught his reflection cast by moonlight atop the water, and the sight gave him pause. He looked a dead man, sleep-deprived and hungry. It'd been only a week, he knew, but even before the castle dungeon he'd been eating poorly, and sleeping little. He cast a pebble across his reflection to scatter it, then stepped in. The water was cold enough to hurt, but he clenched his teeth and fought his shivers. He'd endured far greater trials in his faith to his god. He would not falter now. When he finished bathing, he ducked his head under completely, feeling the chill seep into his bones, shocking the exhaustion from his veins. When he emerged, his entire body shook, but he did not care. After putting his clothes back on, he walked to Velixar.

The prophet smiled, and his red eyes seemed to glow brighter. He gestured to the open chest.

"Put on your armor."

Darius did so one piece at a time, showing no hurry. The water had left him numb, and his shivers lessened with every minute. In the light of the moon, he felt calm, almost peaceful. If not for Velixar's presence, he might have felt completely at ease. Putting on his armor, etched with symbols to Karak, the Lion, as well as ancient runes proclaiming his might, he felt once more the champion he'd been. Only one thing mattered, and he knew what it was.

Velixar knew as well, and he offered the hilt of Darius's sword.

"Karak is not a god of miracles," said the prophet. "You have made but a single step on a very, very long road. I offer you your blade, your means to bring wisdom to this chaotic world. If you accept, you must swear to heed my words as truth, to know that our god speaks through me, and me alone. Do not take this lightly, Darius. Think on it. If you wish, I can return you to your cell, and leave you to the fate this world would bring you."

Darius shook his head. He would face this future, reveal the truth of his god. There would be no return to a prison, not outward, not within.

"My sword is my soul," he said, stepping forward and taking the handle. "And it has always belonged to Karak."

Exhilaration shot through him as his fingers closed about the leather. The dark fire was not much, just the faintest shimmer even newly anointed paladins could outmatch, but to Darius it was a brilliant blaze of the greatest significance. It flickered and burned across his blade, unable to survive the weakest of winds. But it was there, and every time the air calmed, it returned. Darius laughed even as tears ran down his face.

"You are beloved in Karak's eyes," Velixar whispered. "Come. It is time we take another step down his road."

He created another portal of shadows, and taking Darius's hand, led him through to the other side. Darius knew not what to expect, nor did he try to guess. For the moment, he was trying to abandon all his previous teachings, to rely only on what appeared to be truth, and what the prophet confirmed. He would accept everything with an open mind, until Velixar failed. A single false word, or moment of doubt, and he would seek Karak in his own way. At least, he thought he might. Feeling the distant touch of his god deep in his chest, and seeing that fledgling fire on his greatsword, made him wonder if he was already decided, his life already bought and earned. His promise to Velixar ... he had not made it lightly.

"Where are we?" Darius asked as they stepped out. It seemed they had not traveled far, for the terrain remained the same, just rocky hills with withering grass and the occasional barren tree. Before him was a heavy cluster of bushes, marking the outline of a small grove.

"Quiet, and listen," Velixar said.

He did, and the sound of moaning reached his ears. Taking a step forward, he pushed through the bushes. Within he found a man lying on his back, bleeding from gashes across his arms and legs. His hands were gone, the bone still exposed. His eyelids were peeled. Despite his training, despite his experience with bloody combat, Darius still found himself on the verge of vomiting.

"What grotesquery is this?" he asked.

"Now is not the time for questions," Velixar said, joining him in the ring. He gestured to the mutilated man. "Do you not understand that is the nature of your failure? You seek answers to things that do not matter. Look at him. Say I found him tortured by bandits and brought him here for succor? Or perhaps he tortured himself, bearing a guilty soul, and he sought me out to help him with his sickness? I might have done this to him myself, but you will never know, will you? Yet you ask, and ask, and do you know what is happening while you do?"

Velixar pointed to the man.

"He suffers. He bleeds. Tell me, does any of that matter in the face of his torment?"

Darius looked into the man's eyes, unsure if the man saw him back. He looked lost in a daze, moaning lightly as he lay there. His stubs shook, and the sight of exposed bone made Darius shiver with unease. The pain ... it had to be excruciating.

"What is it you want from me?" he asked the prophet.

"To learn. To understand. This is one of the greatest lessons I can offer you. Here, now, realize the many paths before you, and then make your choice."

The man jerked back his head, and suddenly his moans turned into bloodcurdling screams.

"What did you do?" Darius asked, having drawn his greatsword without realizing it.

"I was numbing his pain," Velixar said. "But no longer. The choice is before you. I will not intervene."

The sword shook in Darius's hand. He saw the fire upon its blade wither and die. Looking back to the man, he knew the lesson Velixar wanted him to learn. It burned in his gut. He wanted to refuse, to deny its wisdom, but how could he hearing such horrific screams? Lifting his sword, he closed his eyes and prayed for forgiveness from Karak. Down came his blade, right through the mutilated man's throat. He silenced the screams. He ended the pain.

The blood on his blade burned away in dark fire.

"So close," Velixar said in the sudden silence. "But I saw your lips. I heard your prayer. There is nothing to forgive, Darius. Do you not understand?"

"The intent," Darius whispered. "It is all in the intent."

"Your intent was to end pain, to stop suffering. There is no sin in killing. Do not even Ashhur's paladins kill? You must be purer. You must embrace Karak's ultimate truth."

Darius stared at the corpse, and he felt cold fingers, like the touch of a ghost, tracing the curves of his spine.

"And what is that?" he asked, fearing the answer.

"Only in absolute emptiness is there Order, and we serve a god of Order. Follow me once more. We must take another step."

No guilt, thought Darius as he tore his eyes away from the corpse. No forgiveness. Seeking the cause was pointless. He had to react to the way things were. Was that not what he'd always chided Jerico about? Ashhur's paladins fought for a world that didn't exist. He, on the other hand, bled for the real world. But there was no comfort in these words, no strengthening of his heart with such understanding. Instead, he felt another part of himself die.

Burn the sick branches with fire, Darius thought, one of Karak's few axioms. *Otherwise that which might live will also die.*

Just how much of his understanding of the world, of Karak, was nothing but dead branches?

Accepting Velixar's offered hand, he took another step, and appeared at the outside of a log cabin. To either side of him stretched acres of flat land, some recently tilled, some left fallow.

"Where are we now?" he asked.

"There is light in the window," Velixar said, gesturing. "Look through, and tell me what you see."

Darius did, feeling fresh dread clawing at his throat. By candlelight he saw a mother and father through the warped glass, kneeling beside a bed. Wrapped underneath covers was their child, a young boy with hair even redder than his father's. Feeling himself the invader on something private, he looked away.

"I see a family in prayer," he said, the words heavy on his tongue.

"They pray to Ashhur," Velixar said. "Not Karak. Not to any true god. Every night they're tucking their child away with lies and delusions. Do you know what they pray for? Protection. Safety. A long, healthy life for that child. Do you think Ashhur hears? Do you think he acts? We are here, and Ashhur is not. We are truth, and he is falsehood. Another choice before you, Darius. I pray you have learned enough to choose what is right."

"Intent," Darius said again, and his sword hand shook.

"And what would your intent be?" Velixar asked.

"No more suffering. No more fear. Salvation from loss, heartache, betrayal, hunger, and lies."

Velixar's eyes flared with color, as if he could not contain his excitement.

"Are you strong enough?" he asked.

Darius looked to the door. He thought of the nameless family inside, of the wounded man he'd killed, and the desires of his god. In the end, he knew what he must do.

"Please," he prayed to Karak. "Everything I am, I have sworn to you. I will not doubt. I will not disobey. Give me a sign. Show me the way, and I will follow without question."

He opened his eyes, and the dark fire on his blade fully consumed the metal. Prayer answered, choice made, he pushed open the door. The family screamed; the father fought. They died, and the fire burned all the hotter. When Darius stepped back out, his armor stained with blood, he threw down his sword and fell to his knees with a sob. Velixar's hands were on his shoulders, his cold cheek pressed against Darius's as his whole body shuddered with tears.

"We are what the world lacks," Velixar whispered in his ear. "We are what the world *needs*. Banish your guilt. You are no longer one of them. You are better. You are a child in the eyes of Karak, and have been made anew."

Darius heard the words, and with strength born of desperation he clung to them in his mind. All the while, he pushed away the images, the blood. As his heart burned, he thought of Jerico, and how the simple act of saving him had thrust him onto this path.

Damn you, Jerico, he thought as Velixar set fire to the cabin with a wave of his hand. *Damn you to the Abyss.*

"Are you hungry?" Velixar asked.

Darius thought it impossible, but his stomach groaned, and he weakly nodded.

"Very well. Pick up your sword, and we will find you a meal."

Darius grabbed the hilt of his greatsword. Deep inside, in a part of him that felt very small, he hoped it would lack the fire of faith, that it would remain plain steel and nothing more. When he lifted it into the air, it burned strong as ever, and that small piece of him burned along with it, just a dead branch meeting its proper fate.

Jerico spent the morning teaching the men how to hold a sword. It seemed like it should have been the most basic of things, but instead he learned how militaristic his childhood had been, where weaponry and training had been daily rituals.

"Higher, Jorel," he said, readjusting the man's grip. Beside him, Adam clutched the hilt with both hands, his meaty fists dwarfing the metal.

"Just one," Jerico said, "we'll look into getting you a bastard sword, perhaps, but for now, just use one."

"Feels better using two," Adam said.

"It's too heavy using just one," another man, Pat, agreed.

"They're balanced for one," Jerico said, trying very hard not to roll his eyes. "If it feels heavy, it means you need to strengthen your arm, and that won't happen if you keep using two ... Trent, what did I say about your feet?"

Thinking back, Jerico decided he had never given his instructors even a pittance of the respect they deserved. He'd hoped to have the men spar, but getting them to grip the weapon tight, but not too tight, with just one hand, and at the right angle from their bodies, felt like trying to teach a pack of dogs how to dance on two legs. Sure, they could do it, but it wasn't coming natural.

"Seriously, Pat," Jerico said, turning back. "Stop crossing your legs!"

"I got to piss," Pat said, looking ashamed.

Jerico opened his mouth, then closed it, realizing he had no clue how to react. He wanted to ask why he hadn't said so, why he'd waited, why he hadn't just wandered off, taken care of business, and come back. Instead he gave him a dumb stare, then waved a hand.

"Hurry up," he said, praying for the hundredth time for patience.

"When we get to spar?" Griff asked.

Jerico caught him giving Adam an evil look, and he knew then and there that when the twins sparred, both would end up needing stitches for days.

"You get to spar when I know neither of you will kill the other," Jerico said, harsher than he meant.

"Hey Jer, like this?" another man asked, and Jerico rushed down the line to double-check. Everyone was shifting about, trying to make things perfect. The paladin kept seeing a hundred things wrong, and it felt like the past half hour had been nothing but fixing error after error after error ...

"Goddamn piece of shit!" Pat screamed from further into the forest. Jerico spun, grabbing his mace. From the corner of his eye, he saw the men turning with him, several nearly cutting their neighbors or dropping their blade from the sudden, surprised reaction. He nearly felt like crying. Not much more than farmers, Kaide had told him before they started. No kidding.

Pat came rushing back to them, but instead of being under attack, he was running as fast as he could while trying to remove his shirt and pants.

"What's going on?" Jerico asked, baffled.

Then the smell hit.

"Skunk!" Adam and Griff swore in unison.

"Damn, Pat, you go and piss on one?" asked Jorel.

Jerico pressed his nose shut with his fingers, his eyes watering at the smell. As Pat neared, the rest gave way, not wanting to get too close.

"What is going on out here?" Kaide asked, stepping out from his cabin. He frowned, sniffed, and then pulled his shirt up to his nose. "Damn it, Pat, a stream's southwest of here. Get in it, and don't come out until you see the moon."

"Sorry," Pat said, his eyes running, his face red. The rest of the men were laughing at him, and Jerico couldn't help but chuckle, no matter how bad he felt for Pat.

"Can't you do something about that?" Kaide asked, joining Jerico's side.

"I can heal broken bones and torn flesh," Jerico said, rubbing his nose. "But that evil is beyond me."

They both laughed, and were still laughing when they heard the sound of hooves thundering across the ground. When they saw the pale look on the rider's face, their laughter died.

"Him!" the man screamed, pointing at Jerico. "He did this!"

Jerico looked to Kaide, and he shrugged, not understanding.

"Calm down, Ned," Kaide said, offering his hand to help the man dismount. Ned did so, still glaring at Jerico. When the paladin neared to listen, Kaide shot him a look, so he stepped back until he was out of earshot.

"Enough practice," Jerico said, realizing the rest of the men were still lingering about. "Take a break, and put your weapons away. Carefully!"

As they scattered, muttering amongst themselves, Jerico watched Kaide's face. Outwardly he showed little sign, but his eyes hardened, and his whole body turned rigid. At last he hugged the rider, then approached Jerico, who didn't fail to notice the man's hands balled into fists.

"What's going—"

Kaide struck him in the mouth, then kicked the back of his sore knee. Jerico went down, screaming in pain. The bandit leader landed on top of him, an elbow crushing his throat.

"You bastard," Kaide said, his voice quiet, cold. "You just couldn't leave things be, could you? Always have to interfere."

"I don't understand," Jerico said, his words cracking.

"You will. You're coming with me to Stonahm. I'll let you see what a fucking mess you've made."

Word spread to the rest of the camp, but given how limited they were on horses, only one other could go with Kaide and Jerico, the short man, Barry.

"Is my family all right?" he asked Ned as they saddled up. "Tell me, is she all right?"

The rider refused to say, even when Barry grabbed him by the shoulders and screamed in his face.

"Look me in the eye!" he cried, shaking him. "Why won't you look me in the damn eye?"

It'd taken two men to pull him off. Now he rode behind Jerico and Kaide, head down and refusing to say a word. The hours crawled, and when they stopped to let their horses rest, not a shred of conversation was spoken between the three. As they neared Stonahm, there was no denying the cloud of smoke in the sky, nor where it was rising from.

"She's all right," Ned said upon seeing the smoke. "I know it. She's all right, and my boys, too."

Kaide's glare was cold enough to freeze the skin on Jerico's neck.

Jerico felt some relief as they finally rode into the village. The smoke was only from a few homes, not all of them as he'd initially feared. People milled about, looking as if they'd just survived a battle. Seeing Kaide's approach, they began to gather.

"Jess!" Barry screamed. "Where's Jess!"

Two boys pushed through the crowd, and they leapt into Barry's arms as he dismounted. Jerico remained on his horse, feeling lost. People were shouting and crying all at once, a mixture of anger and heartbreak. Kaide tried to soothe them, but soon gave up.

"Where's Beth?" he asked repeatedly. "I said where's Beth?"

"With the others," said a farmer. "Kalgan's looking over them."

"Come on," Kaide said. Jerico dismounted and followed, leading his horse behind him.

The wounded had been too many to fit into a single hut, so they lay spread out on blankets in the open air. Jerico feared to count how many. Kalgan walked among them, his clothes and hands coated with blood. When he saw their approach, he looked at them with dull, expressionless eyes. In the corner, Barry wept over the still body of his wife while his two boys clutched him tightly.

"Kaide," Kalgan said, shaking his head. "I don't know what to say."

He pointed to where Beth sat on the blankets, staring into nowhere. Kaide called her name, and when she saw him, she burst into tears. Jerico stood, feeling the intruder, as the father ran to his daughter.

"Do you remember what I said?" Kalgan asked, trying futilely to wipe his hands on his robe. "Do you remember?"

"I do," Jerico said, feeling a knot swell in his throat.

"Good. I hope you remember until the day you die."

Kalgan went on his way. Jerico looked about. He saw at least seven dead, and thrice that wounded. On every street at least one building had been burned, and in the distance, he saw the torched remains of an entire field of crops. The lump in his throat swelled, and he had to struggle to keep his hands from shaking. After a horrific wait, Kaide finally kissed his daughter's head and returned.

"You attacked one of Sebastian's knights," Kaide said, his glare full of fire. "You struck him, beat him down, and then sent him on his way. You damn fool, this is what you've done."

"He was going to rape-"

"I don't care!" Kaide shouted. "One woman? One rape? Do you know what they did here? A hundred knights came with swords and armor, burned their food, took every woman they pleased, and killed whoever resisted. One woman, you fucking paladin, all that to stop the rape of one woman? A hundred women can now blame you. A hundred women ..."

He choked up, and Jerico looked to Beth with newborn dread.

"Even her?" he asked.

There were tears in Kaide's eyes when he looked back.

"Even her."

10

They stayed in the homes of people that would take them. For Jerico, that meant he had none, so he slept in the hut that had been his during his injury. He lay inside, feeling drained beyond belief. He'd knelt and prayed with any who would accept it, but even those with severe injuries seemed hesitant. Normally he would have felt anger, but instead he felt only sadness. Shouting to them how he'd been in the right felt hollow, and selfish. No matter his healing touch, he could not bring back the dead, nor remove the painful memories they'd endured.

"I wasn't wrong," Jerico murmured, trying to sleep. Night had finally come, and no one had been happier to see the rise of the moon than him. Free of his armor, he tried to relax, and force his mind from the hundred horror stories he'd had confessed to him. He tried to forget Barry's wail, forget that single look of betrayal Beth had given him when she'd turned his way. Unable to help it, Jerico felt tears slide down his face.

The door to his hut opened. For some reason, Jerico knew who would be there.

"Close the door," he said. "I would hate for anyone to see you like this."

Barry stood at the entrance. In one hand he held a bottle, in the other, a knife.

"I ain't afraid of what they'll say," the man said, his speech slurred from the alcohol. "You think I care?"

He stepped further in, and the door shut behind him. Jerico sat up, glancing toward his mace and shield. If he acted quick, he could still retrieve them. But he didn't.

"What are you here for, Barry?" he asked.

"You," he said. He sniffed, and his red eyes were heavy with tears. "My Jess ... they say she ran. The others, the ones that didn't fight it ... but no, Jess ran. Stupid woman, she ran, and now who'll raise my boys? Me?"

He laughed, the bottle swinging loosely in his hand.

"I'm no good. Never been. Was lucky enough to get Jess. Why'd you do it, Jerico? Don't you ever think? Every damn peasant boy knows you leave a lord's knights well enough alone. Boys! But you ... you ..."

He waved the knife, and he took an uncertain step toward him. Jerico remained still, refusing to look away from that pained gaze.

"Are you here to kill me, Barry?"

Barry laughed.

"Maybe. Maybe not. Don't think even the gods know what I'm gonna do, but I know what I *want* to do. I want to jam this knife so far down your throat you choke on my elbow. You were supposed to help us, Jerico. You were supposed to *help* us ..."

Jerico stood slowly to make sure Barry knew he posed no threat. From the corner of his eye he watched the unsteady knife. So far it wasn't poised to stab. Not yet, but close.

"Tell me what you want," he said. "Tell me, so I may grant it."

Barry pointed the knife at him.

"I want you to know you was wrong. I want to hear it from you. I want a goddamn apology. Don't you get it?

This is all your fault, and I won't let you say otherwise. I won't *let* you!"

Jerico took a deep breath. He would not lie, not now, not ever. He doubted anything he could say would comfort him, so he spoke the truth and prayed it would be enough.

"I'm not sorry," he said. "Not for saving that woman. Not for doing what we both know was right. The only thing I'm sorry for is that I wasn't here to protect everyone. That I couldn't have died with my shield on my arm and my mace in my hand, standing against those knights, be they a hundred or a hundred thousand. I'm just one man, Barry. One man, foolish, weak, exhausted, and alone. Take my life if you want it. I won't stop you."

Barry flung his bottle to the ground, where it shattered.

"You think you can talk yourself outta this? You think I won't do it? I will. I fucking will!"

"You won't."

Kaide stepped inside, his dirk drawn. He glanced at the broken bottle, then at Jerico.

"Go back to your boys, Barry," Kaide said. "I'd hate for you to do something you'll regret for the rest of your life."

Barry wavered, and he looked like a mouse caught between two cats. The knife shook in his unsteady hand.

"He ain't worth it," he said, putting away the knife. His shoulder bumped into Kaide's as he walked out of the hut. "I thought he was, but he ain't."

Kaide watched him go, then shut the door behind him.

"Thank you," Jerico said.

"Forget it. He's right, you know? You don't tease a boar, then turn your back to it. You let this entire village suffer, and for what? So you could play the hero? Feel better about yourself? What you stopped happens every day in every single village across Dezrel. It's shit, it's wrong, but so's a hundred other things. We close our eyes, clench our teeth, and endure until we have the strength to fight back."

"You ask the impossible, Kaide. If I see an innocent suffering harm, I'll stop it. I won't keep my hands still because I fear the reactions of an evil world."

Kaide rolled his eyes.

"Such prepared, proud words that don't mean shit. We're not you. What do you think would have happened if this village had fought back?"

"I have no delusions," said Jerico. "I'll die one day, probably soon, and it'll be defending someone without the strength to defend themselves. Just because I die doesn't mean it was wrong to do so. If your private war against Sebastian never succeeds, does that mean you were wrong to fight him? We must fight, and fight, so that this dark world knows hope. One day, maybe it will even know victory. I pray to Ashhur it does."

Kaide crossed his arms and looked away. His voice softened.

"This is as much my fault as yours either way. If not for my rebellion, Sebastian might have ignored this, or only sent a few to find out who had struck at the knight."

Jerico put a hand on Kaide's shoulder.

"Blame the evil on those who committed it," he said. "Not yourself. Not others. Sebastian sent the knights, and the knights themselves burned, looted, and raped. If you must feel wrath, then direct it at them."

Kaide looked at him with an expression akin to wonder.

"Do you really feel no regret? No remorse? Are you not even human?"

Jerico chuckled, even though he felt ready to collapse from his exhaustion.

"I do. More keenly than you could know. I could have protected her, Kaide. Beth wanted to come with me, but I refused. I told her to remain here. When the knights came, when they ... she could have been safe. I was angry. Bitter. I should have said yes. I should have ... the way she looked at me, she knows it, too. I'm sorry, Kaide. I should have stayed. I could have given myself up, and spared the rest of the village."

"And not fought?"

"I'll die to protect others. If that is what it would have taken, then yes."

The bandit leader walked to the door, and he rested his weight against it as he thought.

"You confuse me, paladin. But at least I know I can trust you. This is the last straw. Sebastian's gone too far. Stories of this will spread throughout the North, and we must fan the flames of rebellion while we still can. Tomorrow morning, we ride. I have one ally, and he must be spurred into action. The time for secrecy and stealth is over."

"And who is this ally?" Jerico asked.

Kaide glanced at him, a tired grin on his face.

"Arthur Hemman, Sebastian's disgraced brother."

Barry remained behind to oversee the rebuilding efforts, as well as bring in more men from the forest hideout. Food would be scarce, but Kaide had kept a small amount of gold from being distributed, and he told Barry to use all of it to prevent them from starving.

"No loved one of mine goes hungry," he had said before they rode northwest. "Not now. Not ever again."

They packed light, Kaide insisting they could fill their packs on the trip there.

"I've given nearly every village at least one satchel of gold," he said as they rode. "If there's a man more beloved in the North than I, I'd like to meet him."

"Nothing says loyalty like stolen coin," Jerico said. Kaide glared but let the matter drop. He was right about the supplies, Jerico soon found out. They stopped at three different villages, and the men and women warmed immediately to their presence when they heard Kaide's name. After the third, they avoided the towns, for their packs overflowed with waterskins and salted meats, and Kaide wanted no more risk of Sebastian hearing of his ride.

"Where is it we go?" Jerico asked near the end of the first day as they stopped at a spring for their horses to rest and drink.

"They call it the Castle of Caves," Kaide said. "Though it's more a prison than anything. Arthur's been holed up there for years, wary of guests and allowing in only those he approves. Always living in fear of his brother's assassins, though I've heard only rumors of any actual attempts. Arthur's never done anything outward to give Sebastian justification for open battle between them."

"You said Arthur's disgraced. How so?"

Kaide stroked the neck of his horse, who was still breathing heavily from the ride.

"Not sure. He's the older brother, and should have inherited the Northlands instead of Sebastian. Something ill happened between Arthur and his father, right before he died. I don't know what, and there's plenty of rumors saying Sebastian's actually to blame. The wealth and power passed over him. Arthur could have fought for it, but instead he retreated to his castle. It wasn't until I came to him, revealing Sebastian's dishonorable actions in Ashvale, that he agreed to help me in any way."

"Will he do so now?"

Kaide chuckled.

"He wouldn't even give us steel weapons for fear they could point back to him. He's a careful man, but I feel there's honor in him. I'm hoping you can instill a bit of fire into his heart, since you paladins seem talented at that. I don't want secrecy any longer. I want a war."

"You're certain he should have been the rightful lord?"

"Without a doubt," Kaide said.

Jerico nodded.

"Good enough for me. Let us hear what he has to say."

They continued northwest, toward the great ocean that formed the western edge of all of Dezrel. The ride was long, two weeks of hills broken by intermittent forests. At least the road was well-cared for, and remained so by the many people they encountered on their way.

"Plenty of trade in the North," Kaide had said at one point, after they'd sneaked off the path to remain unseen by a large caravan guarded by Sebastian's men. "Our towns practically survive off it. Makes the winters particularly harsh."

"Durham was the same," said Jerico. "But we at least had the river."

"No rivers here," Kaide said, his knife hand twitching at the sight of the loaded wagon. "Just blood and gold."

Twice more they had to shy off the path as they approached the Castle of Caves, through no fault of Sebastian's. Men, either dark paladins or priests, rode with the standard of Karak upon their horses. Jerico kept off the road, watching them pass.

"I never heard reason for our hiding," Kaide asked one night as they camped.

"All forces of Karak hunt for my kind," Jerico said, the words foul on his tongue. "I fear I'm the last. The Citadel has fallen, and with it went the vast bulk of my order. Whoever is left is like me, alone and in hiding."

"You're terrible at hiding, then."

"I'm at the side of bandits. Who would look for a paladin there?"

Kaide laughed.

"Now I wonder ... how much of a reward could I get for turning you over? I'm a good barterer. Maybe I could fund an entire mercenary army with what they'd pay, especially if you're the last."

Jerico threw his bread at him.

"You're not amusing."

Kaide shot him a wink.

"If you say so."

At a fork in the road, they traveled west instead of north. The path immediately grew wilder, much of it covered with a thin layer of dying grass. The land, which had evened out for a few miles, once more rose into many clusters of hills. Atop the tallest loomed a castle built of gray stone.

"That it?" Jerico asked, pointing.

"That's it."

Before they could reach the gate, a patrol rode out to meet them, four men on horseback. They appeared on edge, but kept their swords sheathed as they formed a circle about them. Their crimson armor bore the standard of the Hemman family, except the rose was violet instead of yellow.

"What brings you to the caves?" asked their leader.

"I've come for a stay in your dungeons," Kaide said, all smiles. "Tell your lord the man from Ashvale comes, and has brought a guest."

The gruff man seemed unimpressed.

"Keep your weapons at your sides," he said. "If you want to see our dungeons, them come with me."

Instead of leading them to the main gate, they veered off the path at a hurried pace. Jerico wondered what was going on, but then the horsemen pulled up.

"My thanks for the escort," Kaide said, kneeling down in the grass. "Take care of our horses, will you?"

His hands searched, and then he lifted up a trap door hidden underneath a layer of dirt. Jerico looked around, realizing the men had them surrounded and hidden with the bodies of their horses.

"Tight fit with your armor," Kaide said, sitting down and then sliding in feet first. "I trust you'll manage."

And then he vanished into the tunnel. Tightening the straps that held the shield against his back, Jerico took a deep breath and then followed. The tunnel was steeper than he expected, and he more fell than crawled into it. When his feet touched solid ground, the trapdoor closed above them. In the darkness, they heard thuds as the men covered up the entrance.

"No torches," Kaide said. "Not for a while. Just take careful steps, and keep your hand against the wall."

Instead, Jerico pulled his shield free and held it before him. The blue-white light bathed them both, easily illuminating the tunnel.

"Hrm," Kaide said, raising an eyebrow. "That works too."

"Lead on," Jerico said. "I'd hate to keep our gracious host waiting."

"Keep the sarcasm to a limit," Kaide said as he walked ahead, his left hand still touching the wall as if he feared the light of Jerico's shield could fade at any time. The whole while, the floor slanted sharply downward. "Arthur's not much for joking of any kind. Terribly serious man, but not much to do about that now. He's always had me come through this tunnel ever since I began my raids on Sebastian's men. Like I said before, he's a careful one."

"Is this cave natural?" Jerico asked, inspecting the walls closer.

"This one? Probably not. There's at least twenty tunnels I know of. I'm sure the early ones were, but even those have been worked and extended. In the span of minutes, the entire castle could vanish underground, and I pity the poor sods stuck trying to chase after them."

Around a curve the tunnel expanded immensely. They entered what seemed like a great hall of an underworld king. Stalactites, some at least twenty feet in length, stretched from the ceiling like teeth in the jaws of an ancient beast. In the light of his shield, the rocks sparkled, showing a hundred different crystals Jerico had never before seen. On either side of their path the stone ended abruptly, and Jerico's light could not pierce the darkness below. The stone bridge had a single rope running across its center, both ends firmly nailed, and Kaide grabbed it to steady himself.

"Step carefully," Kaide said, and he laughed at Jerico's blank stare. "What? You aren't afraid of a little fall, are you?"

Jerico glanced into the chasm, and a shiver ran through him.

"Not before today," he said.

"Put your shield away if you'll feel better. Just use the rope to guide you."

"I'd rather see."

The bandit shrugged.

"If I was to fall to my death, I'd prefer not to see the ground coming. Up to you, though."

The paladin ground his teeth.

"You're not helping."

Kaide walked along the stone bridge across the chasm, eventually vanishing beyond the reach of the shield's light. Praying to Ashhur for the steadiest footing known to man, Jerico began crossing. The bridge was several feet wide, and it felt sturdy enough when he stepped. But the stone itself was wet, for water dripped from ceiling as if it were a lazy rain. The thought of a single slip, a lost grip on a rope, all leading to a very, very long fall ...

"You still alive?" Kaide called out, his voice echoing.

"Yes," Jerico said, unable to muster a worthy retort to such a stupid question.

Halfway across he felt something smack against his shoulder. He immediately froze, and had to choke down his cry so Kaide would not hear. It was a rope, just a rope, though what it hung from he had no clue. Deciding that just for once they could have used the front gate, he continued. When reaching the other side, Jerico hurried the last few steps, beyond relieved to be inside another, much smaller, tunnel. Kaide clapped him on the back, then pointed back toward the bridge.

"Feel that rope?" he asked. "When I first came here, I was told that if you pulled it and held, it'd collapse enough stones from the ceiling to crush the bridge into a thousand pieces. Like I said, I pity the fools trying to give chase through here."

Jerico pushed further ahead into the tunnel, wanting nothing more to do with the chasms. He hoped Kaide didn't notice the slight shaking of his shield as he held it aloft for light.

"How much farther?" he asked.

"Not far."

Sure enough, the cave angled upward, then ended with an iron door. There was no handle of any kind, and when Jerico pressed against it, it lacked the slightest give.

"Locked and barred from the inside," Kaide explained. "Just in case someone gets too clever. Bang on it a few times. The jailor will hear."

"Jailor?"

Kaide looked at him as if he were dimwitted.

"I said we were visiting the dungeons, didn't I?"

Jerico struck the door with his fist, hurting his ears with the loud clang of his platemail striking metal. After a wait, and an impatient gesture from Kaide, Jerico did so a second time.

A tiny slit in the door opened up, letting in a beam of light that fell upon Jerico's breastplate.

"The man from Ashvale," Kaide said, stepping in front of the paladin. "And a friend."

"You know the password?"

"I know you, One-Eye, and you know me. Now open the damn door."

"Was that the password?" Jerico asked as the slit shut, and they heard a heavy thud as the bolt on the other side was removed.

"Nah. I just like messing with One-Eye. One time he kept me waiting for an hour while he tried to convince Arthur that the king of Mordan was down here."

"Why'd he think that?"

"Because that's who I told him I was."

The small, circular door opened, flooding the tunnel with light. Kaide exited first, then offered Jerico a hand. As the jailor dropped the door shut behind him, Jerico took in his surroundings. Sure enough, they were in a dungeon, albeit a small one. He saw only two cells, and both were empty. The walls were packed dirt instead of stone. The jailor himself was an ugly man with, true to his name, only one eye. The other was missing, and without an eye patch, the vacant slot made his face all the more grotesque.

"Is milord expecting you?" One-Eye asked.

"I don't know. Should we go ask him if he is?"

One-Eye scratched his head.

"Guess that's all right. You go find out if he is. I'd hate to bug him if he ain't."

"That's a good man," Kaide said, smacking One-Eye's shoulder with an open palm. "Stay sharp. I heard something big following us in the tunnel. I think it's a dagadoo."

"You seen it, too?"

One-Eye clutched his club tightly with both hands.

"I heard it. You can, too, if you listen quietly enough. Come on, Jerico."

Kaide led him toward the stairs out of the dungeon.

"Dagadoo?" Jerico asked.

Kaide shrugged.

"He's been hunting it for a year now. One-Eye's a half-orc, you know."

Jerico glanced back at the big lug, who crouched atop the closed tunnel door with his ear pressed against the metal.

"Does that explain the ... you know ..."

"That and more."

Two guards stood at the top of the stairs, each holding a spear. They appeared to have been waiting for them, and without a word, one gestured for them to follow. They walked through the castle, which appeared plain and open compared to the earthen beauty of the caverns. At last they reached the lord's hall, which was just the throne, two benches, and many, many guards.

"Kaide," the lord of the caves said upon their arrival, standing to greet the man.

"Arthur," Kaide said, bowing low. Jerico did likewise.

Arthur was a tall man with a heavy beard. When he stood, it was with the perfectly straight posture of a man who had spent years among fighting men. His green eyes were youthful, though his beard betrayed a hint of gray.

"I see you have brought a guest," Arthur said, his deep voice booming in the enclosed room. "Greetings, paladin of Ashhur. I ask the privilege of your name."

"Jerico of the Citadel, your grace."

"The Citadel? I've been hearing rumors of its collapse. Is there any truth to the matter, or are the peasant-folk spreading lies?"

"No lies," Jerico said quietly. Arthur's face softened.

"Accept my condolences. No man should lose his home. Perhaps some other time you may tell me the story of how it happened, if you even know it."

"If you wish, milord."

"Forgive me for the intrusion," Kaide said, "but matters have pressed me beyond courtesy. Sebastian has gone too far, Arthur. His knights descended upon Stonahm, killed many, burned our crops, and raped our wives and daughters. Twice now he has brought ruin to my home, and I will stand for it no longer."

Arthur sat down on his throne, plain wood stained a dark brown. His hand stroked a crease in the wood, a habit of thought.

"I have never denied my brother's occasional brutality," he said, sounding distracted.

"But this is beyond that. This was unprovoked, nothing but a vicious display to enforce his rule. Stories of it should be reaching your hall very soon, if they have not already. I've sown with gold and coin a hundred seeds of rebellion, and now is the time for them to sprout. The people are ready to rise against him. They just need a name, a leader to call them to action."

"And I wonder, why is that not you?" Arthur asked, leaning back in his chair. "The common folk love you. They tell stories of such generosity that show either they are mad to believe them, or you are mad to have done them. You would have me depose my brother, and then what? Set you up as a lord of some sort? Hand the realm over to you, so I may return to my caves? Or will those same people yearning for rebellion find the stories changed, so that I am now the villain?"

"I seek vengeance against Sebastian," Kaide said, struggling to remain calm. "That is all I desire. You know this."

"Aye, I do. And I know that vengeance is blinding, and once it is met, a hole remains. What will you see when your sight returns?"

"I'll see my daughter," Kaide said softly. "The one Sebastian's men ravaged only two weeks prior. My men will lay down their arms, and we will return to our homes. I'll fill that hole you speak of with the love of my Beth, the only child I have left of my precious wife. My wife, whom your brother killed. Do not doubt my loyalty, my aims, or my honor. It is you who should have ruled the North, you who could have prevented all of this. I ask that you do so now."

Arthur pressed his knuckles against his lips as he thought. His eyes flickered between the two of them. Jerico felt the air about him thicken, and the guards seemed nervous. No doubt Kaide speaking of Arthur's denied inheritance was a grievous breach of protocol.

"Sebastian has thrice my number of soldiers," he said at last. "He has all the coin, all the wealth, and all the land. Can your simple villagers make up for that? Can they wield weapons on a battlefield, pay for our food, and lay siege to the Castle of the Yellow Rose?"

The slightest smile curled at Kaide's lips.

"Just because we might not win doesn't mean we are wrong to fight. Claim your inheritance, Arthur."

Jerico's mouth dropped a little. He couldn't decide if Kaide had learned from what he'd said, or simply felt like using it because it furthered his cause. The paladin almost felt betrayed, though he knew it silly to think so.

The words had their effect on Arthur, though, far more than they had on Kaide. The lord sat up straighter in his chair, and he motioned for his guards.

"I will need time to think on this," he said. "For you have given me much to think on. Until then, you will stay as guests in my castle, and have what little comforts I can afford. Sir Cyan, please, take them away."

"With me," said a dark-haired man, stepping from behind the lord's throne. "I'll escort you to your rooms."

Their accommodation was simple, but acceptable, with the two to share a room. They flipped a coin to see who got the bed, Kaide winning. Jerico eyed the coin, suspecting trickery, but Kaide refused to say either way, denying the paladin the chance to know if he spoke truth or lie.

"Do you think Arthur will join us?" Jerico asked as he spread sheets across the cold floor and began taking off his armor.

"He's easily manipulated, so long as you can tug at his sense of honor. Your earlier words did that pretty well, I think."

"Nice to know I was needed."

Kaide chuckled.

"Consider yourself emotional support. That, and having a paladin at my side does wonders to elevate my own status in the eyes of Arthur. Trust me on that. It makes it harder for him to see me as just a rugged, lawless bandit."

"Even if that is what you are."

"You're free to leave at any time."

Jerico fluffed his pillow, then lay down on the floor to test its comfort. It was far from comfortable.

"One day," the paladin muttered as Kaide took out the coin and rolled it across his knuckles, mischief glinting in his eyes. "One day, I'll take you up on that."

11

"Why have we come here?" Darius asked as high above the stars twinkled.

"And you complain of my questions," Velixar said, walking beside him. "Surely you can think of why we return."

Before them stretched the town of Durham, Darius's place of teaching for over a year. It was there he had tended his flock, and there he'd first met Jerico. A hundred memories flooded him as the two walked through the quiet streets. Time had erased the bloodstains, but not the vicious claw marks across the many buildings. Wolf-men had torn through the village, and Darius had stood against them, side by side with Jerico. They'd been heroes, he knew, and his name was retold in stories all throughout the North. He thought of that night, and of the pure calm he'd felt at Jerico's side. There'd been such a wonderful simplicity to it all. The wolves had been his enemy, Jerico his friend, and together they fought until death.

But what would Velixar have called for? And what did he want now?

"Is it because of Jerico?" Darius dared ask.

"Everything we do, in one sense or another, is because of him," Velixar said, frowning. "Because of your failure to kill him, to be exact. If you're to ask questions, learn to ask better ones."

They stopped in the center of town. Darius looked to homes, seeing a surprising number of new ones. After that night, he'd talked with Jerico of the survivors, merely a third of what they had been. Still, they had rebuilt, and now slept in peace, though he wondered how many dreamt of dark shapes crossing the river, yellow eyes glinting ...

"I wish you could sense it," Velixar said, closing his eyes and lifting his arms to the sky. "Even in death, the power of life lingers on. Not just for mankind, either. A shame the bodies of the wolves were burned. They would make excellent servants for Karak."

They reached the center of town, and there Velixar stopped. He seemed too pleased with himself for Darius to feel comfortable. In the distance, wild dogs began howling, as if they sensed the presence of the prophet.

"Do you know why I have brought you here?" Velixar asked.

"I can think of many reasons, therefore I cannot say. Why?"

"You let Ashhur's paladin teach here, unchallenged, unquestioned. You let his lies spread, let his frailties be viewed as strength. Tonight, you shall rectify this error. Call the town. Bring them before you, and in the dead of night, show them truth."

The prophet turned and began walking toward the distant forest that outlined the Gihon River.

"Will you not stay?" he asked.

"This is your test," Velixar said, looking back. "Before the night's end, I will return. Pray I am pleased with what I find when I do."

Darius watched him go, and felt relieved when he was gone. For the first time since the dungeon, he was alone.

Even when he prayed, he felt Velixar's presence lingering like an intruder. At least now he could breathe.

"Rectify my error," he muttered, looking about. "Easier said than done."

In the deep of night, all would be asleep. Time to wake them up. He took his sword and stabbed it into the dirt before him. Clutching the hilt, he harnessed the power of Karak in one of the few ways he knew how. His voice multiplied in volume, thundering over the town as he gave his call.

"To me!" he cried. "To the center! I am Darius, returned, and my news is grave!"

Three times he let out his cry, until certain everyone would hear and obey. No doubt they felt fearful of another attack by the wolf-men. Let them. What waited by the river was far more dangerous than any wolf.

"Darius?" asked a familiar voice. Of the first to arrive was Jeremy Hangfield, the wealthiest landowner of the village. He wore heavy robes tied with a gray sash. At his side was his daughter Jessie, clutching his hand tight.

"Jeremy," Darius said, tilting his head in respect. "I'm glad you've come. I will need your help in convincing the rest."

"Convincing them of what?"

Instead of answering, Darius shouted again, urging the villagers to hurry. He beckoned them closer with his arms. As he spun, he took in the faces, former friends, acquaintances. For a moment, he thought there were still many lagging behind, perhaps even sleeping, but then realized the extent of the damage the wolf-men had inflicted. Two-thirds of the town, Jerico had claimed after taking count that horrible night. So many faces he did not see, and his heart ached for their fate. How many had been of his own congregation? Worse, how many had died with their faith clutching a lie?

"I know you all, as you know me," Darius began. He'd always been comfortable speaking to crowds. He'd even joked with Jerico about how much better than him he was. His faith had given his words a fire the other paladin could not match, but tonight ... tonight, he felt timid, quiet. Once he might have spoken, and trusted his words to be heard, but now he shouted as if he feared the sounds of the night would drown him out.

"I am Darius, paladin of our great lord Karak. I come to you with a heavy heart, and a heavier conscience. Many of you once gathered about when I lectured, and to you, I apologize for my absence. This night will be kindest to you, so do not fear what I have to say. To those who knelt with the paladin, Jerico, it is you whom I speak to with greatest urgency."

"Come inside," Jeremy said, his voice low. "Tell me first what danger wakes us in the night. Don't do this here. You look a man feverish and ill."

"No!" Darius screamed. "I am here because I must be. I have no choice. No choice! The darkness walks this night, and it brings a fire more dangerous than the teeth of wolves. It brings the fires of the Abyss. Forgive me, people of Durham, for my weakness. I let a liar become my friend. I let falsehoods be spoken next to my truths. In cowardice, I did not act, but I must now. Those of you who would worship Ashhur, I tell you: your god is false. What he teaches is lies and delusions, a doctrine made for a different world, not our own. Bend your knee, and swear to Karak. Judgment has come. Do not hesitate. Do not question. Bend the knee!"

Angry murmurs spread through the crowd. Few bowed, and even they seemed upset.

"Enough of this madness," Jeremy said, grabbing Darius's arm. "You disturb our rest for this?"

"Get back!"

Darius shoved him aside, and he pulled his greatsword free of the earth. Its fire burned across the blade, but not just the blade. His blackened hand was consumed as well, a dark flame wreathing his exposed skin, burning away the gauntlet.

"If you will not bow, you must leave tonight!" he cried. "No delay. No waiting. For the sake of your very lives, I demand this of you. Durham belongs to Karak now. If you would still live your lives in chaos, then go elsewhere."

The crowd's anger increased tenfold.

"This is our home!" they shouted. "Our land!"

Darius looked to them, and in their eyes he saw only fear and confusion. Symptoms of chaos.

"Do not misunderstand me," he said. He pointed his blade at Jeremy. "I once lacked courage. No longer. I will slay all those who neither bow, nor flee. No more words. No more arguments. You all have heard, and know I speak truth."

"What's the matter with you?" asked a man, pushing to the front of the crowd. Darius recognized him as Jacob Wheatley, a poor farmer. He held a heavy club in hand, just one of many that had come to his gathering armed with simple weaponry. "Wasn't so long ago you stood here and defended us. You saved us from the wolves, and now you're telling us to leave?"

"You don't have to leave," Darius said.

"Not if we bow. I ain't bowing, Darius. You saved my life, and I owe you, but nobody forces me to do nothing I don't like. Karak ain't my god. If you still say we go, then I might have to use this club here on your thick skull."

"What are you doing?" Darius asked as Jacob tensed, holding the club before him like a sword. "You've seen what I can do. You know I am better than you. What hope do you have?"

"Hope that you'll learn some damn sense."

Darius looked to the crowd. Even those that had bowed, their faith loyal to Karak, had stood. Anger trembled in his breast. This was what Velixar wanted, wasn't it? This was his way, and look what it cost him. The souls he had were gone, and the rest were ready to fight, unknowingly fighting for Ashhur. Or was this another lesson? What would Velixar say when he walked into this unruly mob and saw only enemies? Or would he say anything at all before the bloodshed began?

"I'm saving your lives," Darius said, his voice dropping. "I'm saving your *souls*. For that, I will do everything I must. Bend the knee, Jacob, I beg of you."

Jacob shook his head.

"I won't," he said. "You won't do it. I know you well enough. You won't."

A direct challenge. The others were watching, waiting. None had the armor or weaponry to face him, but with their numbers, they had a chance to bury him if they attacked as one. But that would need bravery, and a communal sense of defense. Damn fools. He would not let them have it. He would not be made a liar. His words were his vow. With a single step, he lifted his greatsword and swung. It cleaved through the club as if it were straw. A second step, and he smashed Jacob in the face with the hilt of his sword. The farmer went down, blood gushing from his nose.

Before anyone could move, Darius put the tip of his blade an inch from Jacob's neck. Even at that distance, the man's skin started to redden from the heat of the dark fire.

"Enough," Darius said, glaring at the crowd. "What else must I do to prove myself to you?"

"You won't," Jacob said, but his voice quivered.

"I will."

"But why? You saved me before, Darius. Don't you remember? Don't you?"

The wolf-man had been on top off Jacob, its teeth already sunken into flesh. Darius had cut off its neck before it could finish, and then taken Jacob back to town. Jerico had then saved his life, with hands that healed. A look at his own hand, and Darius saw only fire. He'd saved Jacob, and now he was ready to kill him.

Once more he looked to the crowd, and he knew not what to say. These were his charges. These were the people he'd sworn to defend. What was it he'd told Jerico? His path was hard, and he didn't always enjoy it. But no parent wished to punish their child. No farmer wanted to cull the weak or ill that might bring down the rest of the herd. As he looked, he saw Jessie staring at him, tears in her eyes. Her father looked ready to explode. The town was uniting, and it was in hatred of him.

"Please," he whispered. "Don't hate me. I do what I must."

What you must? Indeed ...

Velixar's voice floated on the wind, and its sound put a chill into his heart. No time left.

"Go," he said, taking his sword and stabbing it once more into the dirt. "Forget my words. Forget everything. Your lives are at stake. I am not alone, you fools, now run. RUN!"

The urgency in his voice finally sent them moving. At first they only rushed, and he had little doubt that many intended to bar their homes and wait out the night, along with whatever nameless fear he warned them of. But that wouldn't last. Already he heard the sound of deep laughter, and in it was such joy. Darius refused to turn. Refused to look. He heard the sound of an explosion, followed by wood raining down upon the ground. Another, and then another. Screams joined it. All the while, he knelt in prayer to Karak, begging for strength. Begging for understanding. Begging for their souls.

At last Darius stood, tears in his eyes.

All around him, Durham burned. People ran for their fields, ran for the forests. Soon they, too, burned, a great wildfire that blotted out the very stars with its heat and smoke. Velixar walked amid the blaze, a dark prophet come bearing judgment. With a wave of his hand, fire spread. With a few words from his lips, lightning struck, blasting apart feeble wooden structures. More screams, cries for help. Darius pulled free his sword, and as he listened to a nearby woman burn alive, he stared at the fire of his blade, the strength of his faith.

It had lessened, but only a little. His heart felt like a bleeding wound, but he clutched to Velixar's words with whatever strength he had left.

"What this world needs," he whispered, even as his tears fell. Darkness struck him, and he collapsed to one knee. Blinded, he heard a sudden roar, its power overwhelming. Words echoed in his head, coming from everywhere, and nowhere.

We are what this world needs. The time for choice is over. The time for mankind's failure is done. We must save them. We must save them all. Order, my beloved paladin. Bring this world Order.

His blindness left him, and feeling coldly detached, he looked up to the smoke-filled sky. Hovering over the village, like a phantom image in the reflection of a pool, he saw the face of a lion. Karak had come to him, and spoken. The honor left him shaken. The words left him numb.

Looking around, he saw the town he had once saved, now lost to fire.

"Is this your will?" he whispered. "So be it. My faith is great. The road is narrow, and harsh. Few will walk it, but I will. I will follow your prophet. Forgive my frailty, Karak. Forgive my doubt. I am one man, mortal, and weak. But I will be strong. I will remember. We do this for them. Always for them."

Faith in Ashhur was like a plague. A single instance could spread. Only one thing would stop it, and at last he knew the prophet's desire.

Burn the sick branches, Darius thought, fully understanding the gift bestowed upon his blade—upon blades of all paladins sworn to his mighty god.

Burn them with fire.

A knocking stirred Jerico from his uneasy sleep. Before he could sit up, Kaide was already at the door, weapon in hand. He put his fingers to his lips, and then motioned for Jerico to answer. The paladin did so, cracking the door enough to let in the light of a candle held by a servant.

"Milord wishes an audience with you," he said.

"Me?" Jerico asked, still groggy. "Now?"

"Most apologies for disturbing your rest, but yes, I must insist. Dress if you'd like, but do not worry about formality."

Jerico shut the door and gave Kaide a confused look.

"Formality?"

"It'd be a strange trap, and for little reason," Kaide said with a shrug. "I'd go, but just in case, bring your mace."

"I'd rather bring my shield."

The bandit shrugged.

"Whatever. I'm going back to bed."

Jerico flung his shield on his back, clipped his mace to his belt, and then exited the room. The servant gave him a funny look, and when he saw the mace, he frowned.

"No weapons," he said.

"I am no threat to your lord," Jerico said. "If you wish, you may ask him."

This didn't seem to appease the wiry servant much, but he gestured for the man to follow. They wound their way through the halls of the castle, which felt more like interlocking caves than hallways. After many turns, they came upon an area of the castle in the open air. Arthur sat on a bench carved of stone, staring at the moon.

"Milord," said the servant, "the paladin wishes to keep his shield and mace. What say you?"

"Fearing assassins?" Arthur said, and he chuckled. He was in his bedrobes, and he gestured to his flimsy attire. "I assure you, I am little threat."

"It is not you I fear," Jerico said, "nor your men. The world is no longer safe to my kind, no matter where I go, but if you insist I will return to my room and lay down my arms."

Arthur waved him off.

"Come. Sit with me in the moonlight."

Jerico did, still unsure of the reason for their meeting. The bench was long, and surprisingly comfortable. The air was chill, for no torches burned nearby lest they obscured the stars. Jerico crossed his arms to keep in his heat.

"Sleep refuses to find me," Arthur said, his head leaned back so he could gaze at the sky. "And if I cannot sleep, then the petty part of me refuses to let others. I could use a man to talk to, Jerico. Someone honest. They say that paladins of Ashhur are incapable of lies, that your god would strike you dead for even the lightest fib. What say you to that?"

"I'd say you repeat children's stories. I speak truth by choice, Arthur, not by fear of lightning bolts from the sky."

Arthur chuckled.

"It must be grand to have all your answers given to you. To the Abyss with politics and fiefdoms. What Ashhur says, you do. You're not much different than any of my knights, are you?"

This time it was Jerico's turn to chuckle.

"If Ashhur gave me orders in the same way you order your knights, perhaps it would be so easy. But even if he did, it would not truly make a difference. If you ordered your knights to abandon their families, and march to their deaths, how many would do so?"

"All of the good ones."

"And how many is that?"

Arthur's smile widened.

"Not nearly enough. But what of you? How much would you sacrifice?"

"All that I have," said Jerico.

"Hrmph. Easy to say, of course. Middle of the night, everything's calm, and every foe is a hundred miles away. But what do you do when confronted with such a terrible choice? What do you do when honor tells you one thing, and your gut tells you another?"

Jerico shifted, and he turned his attention from the stars to the troubled lord.

"What bothers you?" he asked.

Arthur sighed.

"You and your friend come to me demanding action, as if it is that simple. You're simple people, of course, a paladin who worries only of his god and a bandit who thinks only of his vengeance. I have no god. I seek no vengeance. I must do what I think is right, not just for me, but for the people of my lands."

"Well," Jerico said, gesturing to the empty surroundings. "You dragged me out here to talk, so let's talk. Help a simple man out. Either that, or let me go back to bed. I'll kick Kaide out here to tell you a few stories."

"Kaide bores me," Arthur said, motioning for a servant to bring him something to eat. A young woman appeared, blonde-haired, carrying a tray of sliced fruits. Arthur took a plate, and told Jerico to take what he liked. The paladin grabbed half an apple and began absent-mindedly chewing it.

"Kaide is ... he's like a rabid dog at times," Arthur said, eating a handful of grapes. "He'd tell me to send every soldier I had rushing the gates of my brother's castle, to the Abyss with whether or not we'd win. He'd slit my throat in a heartbeat if it got him to Sebastian. Advice from him is pointless. I know what he wants, and what he'll say. But you ... To be honest, paladin, I haven't a clue why you're with him. It sounds like the makings of a very bad joke."

"A bandit and a paladin, into a tavern they go," Jerico said, and he laughed. "And your guess is as good as mine what the next line might be. I help because I feel I should. Kaide might be willing to go too far for what he wants, but at least his cause is just. Your brother's actions against him ... there is no excuse for murder and bloodshed done in the name of greed."

"Greed is a tricky thing," Arthur said. "Might not greed guide my own actions here? What if I care not for righting my family's wrongs? What if I want power, and will use a misguided, homeless bandit to further my ends?"

"If you have that fear, Arthur, then you are most certainly not that kind of man."

Arthur scratched at his beard.

"I forfeited my right to my father's holdings. Honor would say I keep to what I did years ago. What Sebastian has done ... it is foul, yes, but is war any better? He's killed a few, but hundreds will die if I muster my men, and the peasant folk, to fight for me."

He sighed and fell silent. Jerico gave him time to think, but when it seemed apparent he would not continue, he prodded him with another question.

"Why did you forfeit your right as firstborn?" he asked. "Whatever you speak stays with me, and you may refuse if you wish. I only ask so that I may help, if I can."

Arthur tossed the rest of his grapes to the floor, and he rubbed his eyes.

"I lose more sleep over that than anything else, paladin. My father was getting old, and his mind was failing him. I pray you never endure anything similar. A cruel fate, watching a proud, intelligent man torn down piece by piece, until nothing is left but a child. There were times he was still himself, but mostly ... Anyway, I talked with a servant I trusted, and procured a simple poison. It would only make him sleep for a few days, that is all, but I hoped that during that time I could take control of my birthright. But I was caught, turned in by that very same servant. My father would hear no reason, for never did he believe his mind was breaking."

Outwardly, Arthur remained calm, as if his face were that of a statue instead of a living man. His voice kept steady. But his eyes were watering, and he made no pretence at hiding it when he wiped them.

"He went to his grave thinking I had tried to kill him, all because I didn't want to wait the few months it would take for him to grow bedridden. The way he would look at me ... so angry, so confused. He was like a child even then, a child betrayed. Father almost ordered me hanged, but Sebastian intervened. If I would only return to my private lands, and relinquish any claims to my inheritance ..."

He looked to Jerico, as if surprised he'd said as much as he had.

"I lost much because I tried to take what was not yet my own. Sebastian rules. The land is not mine. Should I spill so much blood for a few farmers and outlaws?"

Jerico crossed and uncrossed his arms, trying to think through his tired, hazy mind.

"I think ... I think I could use a drink," he said.

"A sound plan."

Arthur gestured, and the blonde serving girl returned, this time holding a tray with two cups and a steel pitcher. Jerico accepted a cup, and he squinted at the liquid the girl poured into Arthur's.

"Do you not drink wine?" the lord asked.

"Water, please," Jerico said, putting the cup back on the tray. The girl smiled at him, but something about her look prickled the hairs on his neck. It wasn't that she seemed frustrated or angry. No, her face remained absolutely, perfectly controlled, if not pleasant. Like glass. Impressive for a servant girl forced awake to attend her lord halfway through the night ...

"Wait," Jerico said, grabbing Arthur's cup with one hand, and the girl's wrist with the other.

"I've change my mind," he said. "Please, drink with me, Arthur."

"Of course," said the serving girl, smiling sweetly at him.

Jerico accepted his cup, and once it was poured, he lifted it to his lips. Immediately he felt the warning of Ashhur sound in his mind. He looked to the girl, who stood perfectly still, as if waiting for her dismissal.

"Arthur," he said, lowering the cup. "Can you please tell me her name?"

"Her, why that's ... step into the starlight, girl, I can't see you well enough without."

As the moonlight fell upon her beautiful features, Arthur's face hardened, and that look alone told Jerico that she was a stranger.

"Don't run," Jerico started to say when she pivoted, smacking him across the head with the metal tray. He rolled with the blow, desperate to remain beside Arthur. Upon hitting the ground he spun, kicking his leg out. The girl leapt, and his leg smacked against the hard stone of the bench. He screamed.

"How dare you!" Arthur roared. "Guards!"

Guards wouldn't be there in time, Jerico knew. Her hand shot out, chopping Arthur's throat. His cry for guards choked down, and blood dripped from his lips. The tray clattered to the ground as she drew a dagger, but Jerico would not allow it. Shield pulled free, he lunged, flinging himself in the way. The dagger clanged against it, and the assassin cried out from the pain of contact.

"Do not interfere, paladin," the woman said, taking a step back.

Jerico readied his mace and kept his shield high. He watched her, waiting. Every muscle in her body tensed. Time was not on her side. She couldn't dance about, nor try to misdirect. Her target was Arthur, and so long as Jerico lived, he would stand in the way.

She shifted her weight twice, twisting her extended foot in a way to feint one direction, then leap the other. Jerico nearly fell for it, but at the last moment flung his mace in the way. It struck across her shoulder, and he heard the snap of bone. Despite this, she did not scream, nor stop. A dagger in her other hand, she thrust for Arthur's throat.

Arthur caught her wrist with both hands and wrenched her arm. As she twisted, he kicked out, snapping his heel against her knee. When she crumpled, he kicked again, this time the arm Jerico had wounded. Jerico stepped between them, again ready with his shield, but Arthur pushed him out of the way. As the assassin tried to stand, he smashed his fists into her head.

"I am no fat lord for you to stick like a pig," he said as he kicked her stomach, blasting a cry of pain from her lips. "In my own home, you come with poison and blade? You'll hang, woman, hang!"

She rolled over, her dagger pressed against her own throat.

"Hang a corpse, then," she said before slicing.

Her face contorted in pain as the life left her eyes. Jerico stepped back as the guards arrived, forming a protective circle about their lord. Arthur pushed them aside, and he clapped Jerico across the back.

"I owe you my life," he said. "Any boon, name it, and it's yours."

Jerico looked to the corpse, then shook his head.

"I will name no boon. Just let me return to rest. All I ask of you is that you do what you think is right concerning your brother."

Arthur nodded, and he pointed to the dead woman's body.

"I have lived these past years fearful of an assassin," he said. "But never did I think Sebastian would actually do it. I always doubted. No longer. He wants my head? Then I'll take his. He wants poison in my veins? Then I'll bleed his out on the field of battle. Go rest, paladin, and worry no more. My decision is already made."

Jerico glanced once more at the woman, absently wondering of her real name.

12

There were tears in Valessa's eyes as she rode from the Castle of Caves. Together; she'd insisted they go together.

I can handle a single disgraced lord, Claire had said. *I'll return by morning, and no one will be the wiser.*

But come morning, she was still inside. This might not have caused Valessa to panic. It wouldn't be the first time her partner had had to improvise. But bells signaled a ceremony of some kind, and as the nearby farmers gathered, Valessa had walked among them, her heart in her throat.

"Last night, an assassin tried to take the life of your lord!" Arthur had called out to the crowd from atop the walls of his castle. "She failed, and took her own life. Before she did, she gave one last request. I grant it now."

And with that, he flung a body over the edge, a rope tied about its neck. Valessa covered her mouth and choked down her cries. The rope snapped taut, jerking Claire's lifeless body side to side. No hood covered her face, and her eyeballs popped loose, hanging by red threads from her skull. Valessa's hands shook.

"You bastards," she'd whispered as the rest of the crowd cheered. "You bastards."

"This assassin was sent to me by the one I used to call my brother, but Sebastian is that no longer. He is a fool, and a coward, to send knives in the dark because he fears the slightest threat to his rule. So be it! I reclaim my birthright. I am Arthur Hemman, eldest son of my father, Arthos Hemman, and the North shall be mine!"

But that was not the worst. Standing there beside Arthur was a man she did not recognize, but that did not matter. She recognized his armor, and his strange shield. A paladin of Ashhur. Somehow, someway, one had survived, and no doubt he'd been the one to keep Claire from completing her task. Her rage grew. Both Arthur and this paladin needed to die, but she could do nothing now. Such a simple assignment, Sebastian had made it seem. All so she could take the life of Darius.

As she fled the city, her hatred grew. So many were to blame. Sebastian, for not cooperating. The paladin, for protecting Arthur. Darius, for his failures bringing them to the North in the first place. Arthur, for not dying like he should have, leaving her task unfulfilled. She had enough hate for everyone, and as a gray sister, she had the power to act on her hate.

Torn between finding Sebastian and acquiring reinforcements from the Stronghold, she rode south, knowing she had plenty of time to decide before the roads forked. Come her second night slumbering beside the road, her choice was made for her.

Valessa ...

She startled, instantly alert. She expected a man kneeling beside her, but instead saw only a serpent coiled at her feet. Given the weather, she knew it should have been sluggish, and in hiding, but instead it slithered toward her, its red scales gleaming in the moonlight. When it reached her side, it coiled up once more, and its mouth opened.

Bloodied fangs dripped poison. Valessa swallowed, tensing. She would give it no reason to strike, no reason at all ...

The serpent struck anyway, its fangs sinking into her hand. As its poison flooded into her, her sight vanished, and all sound became the deep whispers of the man in black.

I call you to me, he said. *Your task is at an end, as I have said. Come join us at the seventh altar, near Stonefield. I await you there, with Darius at my side.*

"You've taken the traitor," she said, unsure if he would hear her or not. All her senses were awry, and the sound of her voice was very far away.

Traitor no longer, and to be punished no more. The Stronghold has sent another, and you will hear from him the wisdom of your High Enforcer.

"They believed your lies."

The truth is sufficient, even for one such as I. Do not tarry, gray sister. And tell me ... where is Claire?

The darkness before her eyes seemed to quiver, and her anger flared as she imagined it was the effect of Velixar's laughter.

"She died, I believe killed by a paladin of Ashhur."

The darkness turned to red. As if from a distant land, she felt her right hand throb with pain.

A paladin? Could it be ...? Hurry, Valessa. We have much to discuss.

And then it all was gone, and she startled once more in her bedroll. Rolling up her sleeve, she looked to her hand. Two punctures still bled in her palm, but they showed no sign of venom.

"Damn you, prophet," she whispered as she bandaged the wound. "Surely there are better ways to send your messages."

Probably, but not one that would amuse him as much. She and Claire had openly defied him. For a man who had walked the land for centuries, he was certainly one to have developed a long memory.

Her nights were lonely as she rode, the village of Stonefield many miles southwest. She crossed dying farmlands, and wondered at the madness that would drive a lord to declare war at the onset of winter. He must expect a swift victory, she thought. Sebastian would be wise to hide in his castle ... but he wasn't that wise. If he was, he would have given her what she wanted: Darius's head. Now it would be denied to her, if the prophet spoke true. She feared he did. Every inn she visited told the same story, which somehow traveled faster than her. Arthur Hemman had declared war on his brother, and even now gathered his forces.

On the twelfth night, she rode into the ancient altar. In ages past, it had been a shrine to Karak. Looming over a patch of bare ground, where no grass would ever grow, was a worn statue of a lion reared onto its haunches. Below it was sacrificial ground, no doubt unused for at least a century. Stones formed a ring, and as she stepped inside, she felt cool air brush against her neck. Even now, with the runes carved into the circle long faded, power remained dormant in them, focusing the will of Karak.

At the feet of the lion stood the prophet, Darius at one side, an elder dark paladin she didn't recognize at the other. Valessa did her best to keep her anger in check.

"I received your message," she said, lifting her bandaged hand. "For a man known to haunt dreams, I expected better."

"I needed to ensure you came," Velixar said, smiling. It might have been meant to disarm her, but instead she felt her hands shifting to the hilts of her daggers. No doubt spiders looked that way as they crawled toward their captured prey.

"Welcome, gray sister," said the unknown paladin, stepping forward and bowing on one knee. "I am honored to meet you at last. I am Mallak, third to Carden in succession of High Enforcer. Your name is well-known to me, even if your face is not."

Valessa bowed in return. She recognized his name, for many times she'd received orders from him. Always through proxy of course, hidden notes and trusted servants. A gray sister's stay in the Stronghold was never long, and rarely revealed to other paladins. Should a dark paladin succumb to weakness or lies, it would be the sisters that came for them, after all. Looking at Mallak, she realized she'd always pictured him as older. Despite his gray hair, Mallak had a youthful look to him, ruined only by the many scars across his face. He looked a veteran of battle, and he stood tall and spoke firm like one of his stature should.

Not Darius. His sunken eyes stared at her as if he were within a dream, and she just a phantom he didn't believe in.

"Honored as well," she said, turning her gaze to Velixar. "And so here we are. I assume with Darius still alive that you spoke no lie, and the Stronghold forgave him?"

"Not forgiven," Mallak said, glancing at Darius. "Only that his Tribunal has been put on hold. We will not execute a member of the faithful. It is rare one will fall so far as we believe Darius did, and then be received once more by Karak, but it appears to be the case."

"My faith in Karak has never wavered," Darius said, a bit of life flaring in his eyes.

"Doubt comes to us all," Valessa said. "Just like it does to me now. He killed fellow members of the faith!"

"Members who now reign in the Abyss," Velixar said, putting a hand on Darius's shoulder. "As Darius will one day reign. Your arguments go beyond your station, gray sister. Any further, and you will appear to be questioning the very will of your god."

Valessa fumed but bit her tongue. She nodded.

"So be it," she said. "Then why am I here, or is it only to be reprimanded and sent away?"

"The paladin," Velixar said. "Did you ever learn his name?"

"I did not."

"A shield," Darius asked. "Did he hold a shield that glowed?"

Valessa thought back to Claire's hanging. It'd been morning, and in the sunlight any glow would have been difficult to see, but ...

"Yes," she said. "It looked strange to me then, but that must be it. It glowed, as the enemy's weapons glow."

Velixar turned to the lion statue, and he lifted his arms to the night sky.

"Here," he said, his voice lowering. "This is where we will bring him. At the altar of Karak, he will be sacrificed. Let his blood flow over Darius's sins, banishing them forever. Who then would doubt my student's faith?"

I would, Valessa thought, glaring.

"Then let us go to where the paladin hides," Mallak said, grabbing his greatsword and drawing it. The fire on the blade burned strong, sucking in the starlight so that the darkness seemed to thicken. "You saw him last at Arthur's castle, no?"

"He will not be there, not by the time we arrive. Arthur marches for war."

"Will Jerico go with him?" Darius asked. His eyes remained downcast as he spoke, as if afraid to meet her eye. "If so, we must go to the battle."

"Sebastian has been a loyal friend to Karak," Mallak said. "There is more at stake than one last paladin of Ashhur. We must ensure Sebastian's victory with whatever power we have. With our swords, and the prophet's sorcery, we can turn the tide of any battle to our desire."

"We will need to hurry," Valessa said. "The ride here was long, and Arthur will surely have begun marching."

"It will be many weeks until he reaches the Castle of the Yellow Rose," Velixar argued.

"Sebastian won't stay," she said, shaking her head. "He'll march out. I know it. He's been eager to fight his brother for years. Now he's left his cave, he'll came riding out with his entire host."

"If you are right, we have little time," Mallak said. "Let us rest this night, for I see Valessa is tired. Come morning, we will ride."

"I travel at night," Velixar said. "As will Darius. Rest now, and then follow the main roads. Listen to the whispers of the common folk. They will tell you where the armies march, and where they will meet. As for us, we will always be near."

With that he turned, and Darius followed him away. As the man in black stepped out of the circle, Valessa felt the very air warm, as if Velixar were a fire giving off cold instead of heat.

"I hope I show no disrespect in saying I do not trust him," she said when certain the prophet was far enough away. Mallak tilted his head and looked as if he were examining her.

"Your faith is strong," he said. "And you are wise in many things, but you are wrong to doubt Karak's hand. I have met him only rarely, but every time, he has spoken with wisdom, and cunning. It was he who brought low the Citadel, though the rest of the world hears only the name of Xelrak. He has given us a great victory, and if he assures me Karak has redeemed Darius's soul, then I will believe him."

Valessa shivered as she thought of Darius.

"It still feels wrong," she said. "Did you not see Darius's eyes? He looks like a dead man, or at least diseased."

Mallak led her from the sacrificial circle to where he had tethered his horse at the base of a tree.

"Indeed, he does," said the paladin as he untied his mount. "But he has much to atone for. I'm sure the guilt of his failures weighs heavy on him, and will until he executes the paladin ... what was his name?"

"Jerico."

"Yes, Jerico. With his death, Darius's atonement will be complete."

Valessa accepted his offered hand, and she sat behind him as he rode out to where she had tied her own horse, following her quick gestures to lead him there.

"But what of Nevek? Pheus? Lars? I heard rumors of other dark paladins going missing, too. What of those potential murders?"

Mallak stopped his horse so she could dismount. As she untied her horse, the strong rope wrapped around a low branch, she heard the paladin draw his blade.

"This fire is for healing as much as cleansing," she heard him say. She turned about, and the frightening power in his eyes sent her to one knee. "We lost good men to him, but I will not lose another if he has truly returned. Let him fight. Let him suffer, and walk Karak's hard road. But should he stumble, or turn against all Karak holds dear ..."

He swung the sword once, cutting the tree limb Valessa had tied her horse to. It fell to the ground with a thud, having barely slowed the blade as it cleaved through the air.

"I follow your orders, not those of the prophet," she said, her head bowed. "Speak the word, and I will turn on Velixar himself."

"I know, girl. Now hurry. I saw an inn a mile back, and I would like to sleep on a soft bed while I still can."

She mounted her horse, tightened her cloak about her, and then let him lead the way.

K aide was surprised by Jerico's silence as they rode back toward Stonahm. He'd expected questions, doubt, maybe even rudimentary discussion of battle tactics. But instead the paladin remained lost in thought, and this made him wonder. When required, the two traded their mounts for fresh horses at a nearby village, with every farmer eager to help out with Arthur's war, as they called it.

Arthur's war. Only now did they accept it, even though he'd spent years spilling the blood of Sebastian's men. Sure, they'd given him their support, but only when he dumped bags of stolen gold at their feet. At every village, he told them of the coming conflict, and made a quick speech rallying them to battle before moving on, trusting them to find and link up with Arthur's vanguard.

"We're making good time," Kaide said as they rode out from another village, saddled up on yet another new pair of horses. Kaide's was a chestnut mare, and he liked the beast's energy.

Still Jerico said nothing.

As they camped for the night, only a two day ride from Stonahm, he finally asked Jerico what was the matter.

"You badgered me into talking," he said, grinning at the paladin. "I think it's my turn, now."

"Ashvale," Jerico said, still staring into their fire. "What happens to the people there if we win?"

"When we win, I suppose I'll leave that up to Arthur."

Half a smile cracked on the paladin's face.

"I'm no fool, Kaide. Arthur will give you what you want as reward for helping him sway the people to his cause. What will you ask of him? Will you butcher the people who live there now? Send them away without homes? What?"

Kaide leaned back and tossed another stick onto the fire. He watched it burn as he chewed on his words.

"You want to know what kind of man I am," he said at last. "That's what this comes down to, isn't it?"

When Jerico nodded, he sighed.

"I don't know anymore, Jerico. There was a time I'd have burned down every building with the people inside to reclaim my home. But we've made a new home now. It's only the fire in my gut that urges me on. I may never take back Ashvale, just as I will never bring my wife back to life. But I can hurt the man who did it. I can make him suffer, as I suffered. He took away my home, my lands, and my wealth. I'll do the same to him."

"Revenge is never—"

"Spare me," Kaide said, glaring. "I know what revenge is. I live with it night and day. What will you tell me, that I'll feel hollow inside when I'm done? You're wrong. I'll feel elation. I've lost friends, family, and spilled sweat and blood to achieve what Arthur now marches toward. I'll feel complete, paladin. Does that answer your question?"

Jerico nodded.

"Sadly, I think it does."

He stood to leave, but Kaide stopped him with two words.

"The Citadel."

Jerico glanced over his shoulder, and he stood very still.

"What does that have to do with anything?" he asked.

"You are no different than I. You lost your friends, your home, everything you'd ever known. Would you tell me that, if given the chance, you wouldn't hunt down and kill the man responsible? Would anything I said change your mind?"

The paladin fell silent. Kaide knew he'd struck home. He wouldn't lose a valuable ally, not now.

"You feel it burning in your gut, don't you?" he said quietly. "I know the feeling. Let me give you what you want. The people talk to me, tell me whispers of stories they might be afraid to speak in the daylight. I know the name of the man who destroyed your home. Stay with me, and I'll tell you. Then you can decide for yourself just what type of man *you* are."

Jerico brushed his red hair away from his face, then touched his shield as if needing its strength.

"I'll help you," he said. "I still think you're in the right, and I'll pray to Ashhur that when the battle is done, you'll be a better man than I fear. Just promise me one thing."

"And what is that?"

Jerico looked him in the eye, and there was a force there that made Kaide's throat tighten.

"Never, ever, tell me that name."

"I promise."

"Good." Jerico smacked him upside the shoulder, and he grinned as if a heavy weight had left his chest. "A few days more until Stonahm, yes? I hope you realize that I barely had time to teach your men how to hold a blade, let alone kill anyone with it. You better have something in mind for them other than standing in the front lines when Sebastian's knights come crashing in."

"One of these days you'll stop thinking I'm a fool," Kaide said, tossing a nearby stone at him. It clanked off the paladin's armor.

"One of these days it'll be right do so, but until then, I work with what I have."

Another rock, this one larger. Jerico failed to duck in time, and as he rubbed his eyebrow, Kaide laughed.

"You may be a big lug in armor," he said, "but even this fool knows to strike where a man's weakness is."

"Mine's my forehead?"

"It's big enough."

Jerico smiled.

"When the battle starts, you stay at my side," he said. "I'd hate for you to get killed off on your own."

Kaide shot him a wink.

"We may lose this entire war, and I'll still survive. Trust me on that. I've eaten the flesh of the dead. Sebastian has nothing, *nothing*, that can frighten me now."

13

Jerico felt uncomfortable with the attention lauded upon them as they rode back into Stonahm. People swelled the streets, either cheering or demanding news. Kaide led the way, pushing through until reaching the home where Beth stayed. Within were many members of his bandits, bunking on the floor wherever there was room.

"You've really done it now," Bellok said, the wizard looking positively annoyed.

"Is that so?" Kaide asked, grinning as the rest came up to greet them.

"You started a war without me. I'm disappointed."

The two laughed, and then louder as Adam and Griff wrapped them in bear hugs.

"We get to fight!" they cried in unison.

Jerico slipped to the side, content to let them celebrate. He caught Beth watching him while waiting for her father to be free. He smiled at her, but she looked away. When Kaide called to her, she ran and wrapped her arm around his chest, hugging him tightly. Her stump remained at her side, as if she were afraid to touch him with it.

"We'll need to move out soon," Kaide said after kissing the top of her head. "There's several places the two lords might choose to meet, and I want us there before either side can discuss matters with the other."

"You really think they'd make a truce?" Bellok asked.

"No," Kaide said, his grin ear to ear. "But I want to be there just in case Sebastian sends an envoy. I'll enjoy sending him back in pieces."

"Father!" Beth said, and he kissed her forehead once more.

"Pay no attention to what I say," he whispered. "Now go on to your room and leave us be. You entered this dark world of adults sooner than you ever should have."

She blushed but did as she was told. Jerico watched her exit, wishing for even the tiniest of smiles to soothe his lingering guilt. He received none.

"Jerico," Kaide said, pulling his attention away. "You know more of this than I. We need to march, and prepare supplies. Come give us a list, will you?"

Jerico helped much as he could, detailing necessary provisions to bring with them, from the obvious to the obscure. Kaide frowned as he listened, and rebuked several things they could not get in time.

"We'll make do without," he said. "How many we have with us ready to go?"

"They been comin' in from all over," Adam said. "Burly men, thugs, farmers, rapers. The whole lot's ready to beat some heads."

"Wonderful," Kaide said, his expression anything but. "How many?"

"Three hundred," Bellok said. "And Adam's right ... they're the sort even we might normally turn away."

"Not today. Give them a stick if we have to. We'll club Sebastian down from his castle walls."

Jerico excused himself, feeling no longer needed as they continued. He stepped out into the town, where many still lingered about the home, hoping for any word. Their expressions did not match their earlier joy upon seeing

Kaide, though. He felt the outsider, a necessary tool, and that was all. He thought of the flock he had taught in Durham, and longed for such a connection. Would any care to hear the word of Ashhur from him, or was the word of Kaide, a word of war, the only thing they desired?

"Will Ashhur be with Arthur's war?" a farmer called out as he walked for the village outskirts.

"I pray he is," Jerico said, committing to nothing further than that.

He walked until he reached the pond, and he found the log he'd sat upon when training his leg. It wasn't so long ago, but it felt like a separate age. Sitting down, he grabbed a few nearby rocks and began skipping them across. Finally alone for the first time in weeks, he closed his eyes and listened for the words of his god. All he heard were the soft sounds of the night birds rustling, the blow of the wind through the grass, and the trickle of the small stream feeding into the pond.

"Jerico?"

The paladin looked back to see Beth standing behind him, holding her stump. She looked ashamed, but she met his eye despite the effort it clearly took.

"Yes, Beth?" he asked.

"Can we talk?"

He shifted, and gestured for her to sit beside him on the log. She did so.

"I ..."

She stopped, and Jerico let her take her time. The sun had begun to set, and he watched the colors.

"I'm sorry," she said at last. "I shouldn't be mad. I am, but ... it was so awful, Jerico. They ..."

She'd begun to cry, and he shushed her.

"You have no reason to apologize," he said. "Not to me."

"But you just wanted to help," she said, shaking her head. With her lone hand she wiped at her tears. "I shouldn't be mad, not when you wanted to help. Her name was Sally, the lady you protected. I thought you should know."

"What happened to her?" he asked. "When the knights returned, what did she do?"

Beth looked away, and she shivered as if she were cold.

"She ran. 'Never again,' she kept screaming. Screamed even before they reached the village. They chased her, and she ... she never came back."

Jerico felt the words knife through his heart. He rubbed his eyes with his fingers, feeling a headache building in his forehead.

"All my fault," he whispered. "Damn it, it's all my fault."

"No, you can't think ..."

"Not her, Beth. You. I could have said yes. I could have spared you all of this. I'll never forgive myself. And I can see it in your eyes, that you know it, too."

She fell silent, and already Jerico felt his frustration grow. Beth was only on the cusp of womanhood, barely able to handle her own problems, let alone his. He should have kept his mouth shut, and carried such a burden on his own. That was his purpose in the world, after all. She had enough to worry about besides his guilt.

"I don't mean to be," she said at last. Her arm wrapped around his waist, and she leaned against his chest. Her tears wet his shirt. "I'm sorry. I don't mean to be so angry. The whole time it happened, I kept hoping you'd save me like you saved Sally. It's not fair, blaming you. Please don't hate me for it, Jerico, please."

"I could never hate you," Jerico said. He watched the sun set as he waited for Beth to cry it all out. Every tear hardened his heart against the men who had done such a thing to her. It wasn't right, but he didn't care. Hopefully Ashhur would forgive him, because for once, grace and forgiveness were the furthest things from his mind. But most of all, he felt his guilt and sorrow fading away. If she could forgive him for such a mistake, then that would be enough for him to forgive himself.

"I'm sorry," he whispered. "For everything I've failed at, for letting you, letting everyone, suffer. I handled it horribly, and could have done something to keep that knight from leaving shamed and furious. I'll do better. I'll find a way. Don't give up on me yet."

"I won't," she said as she pulled back, sniffing and turning away as if embarrassed. "Will you help my dad fight?"

"I will, for as long as I believe it right to do so."

"I was there that winter," she said. "What we had to do, it was ... will my father go to the Abyss for it? For ... you know ... what he ate?"

He could see the question in her eyes, the true words she meant to say.

What we ate.

"Ashhur turns no soul away," he said. "No matter the past. It's forgotten. Murderer or priest, pious or thief, all are children in his eyes. I don't think your father will be condemned forever, not for that. And neither will you."

Her relief spread across her face, and she hugged him, this time unworried about her stump of an arm.

"Promise you'll come back to visit?" she asked.

"I promise. And thank you, Beth."

"Cheer up next time I do see you," she said, forcing a smile. "You're much more fun to be around when you're in a good mood."

Jerico laughed.

"I'll keep that in mind. Go on to bed. I need some time alone to pray."

She left, and once more, he felt the sounds of the night envelop him.

"Heed the voices of children," Jerico said as the evening star pierced the hazy purple sky. He focused on it, as if it were Ashhur and could hear every word. "I hope this is what you want. No more doubt. No more worries. I go to war, and I ask your blessing upon it."

He stood and grabbed his shield and mace, which he had put at his feet. The shield shone brilliant in the night, and he smacked the front of it once for reassurance before returning to Stonahm to sleep.

Come morning, he and three hundred others rode west, to where they believed Arthur would be.

Sir Gregane stared at the map of the North and frowned.

"I hate maps," he muttered, pointing at a section of sharp, interconnected triangles. "Is that forest, and if so, how dense?"

His second in command, a knight named Nicholls, leaned over and scratched at his chin.

"I've hunted there once," he said. "The land's mostly flat, and the trees are thick at times. There's many gaps, though, as if the woods and grass couldn't make up their mind who got to grow where. I think that's what the cartographer meant to imply."

The flap of their tent shook in the wind, and Gregane turned and jammed his sword through the fabric, pinning it to the ground.

"The ground is flat," he said, returning to the table. "You're certain of this?"

"As I can be two years after being there."

The two men were alone in the tent, by Sir Gregane's orders. In that privacy, with a man who had once been his squire, he could finally discuss and strategize without fear. Too many were vying for favor in Sebastian's eyes, under the assumption that once Arthur's lands were conquered, a new lord would need appointing to rule. Some were already trying to sabotage his command, or cause greater casualties and delays than there might be otherwise when defeating the renegade brother. It seemed Gregane was the only one who understood Sebastian would appoint no one but himself to rule all of the North.

"What do you truly think?" Gregane asked.

Nicholls shrugged and pointed at the map.

"It'll be difficult for our cavalry to maneuver, depending on where we meet. And they might have ambushes planned, hence why they've chosen the area."

"At least it's far from any town," Gregane said, still staring at the map as if he might bore a hole through and see into Arthur's mind. The lord had sent a rider, alerting Gregane and his commanders that Arthur sought to meet on a field of battle, in the area known to the locals as the Green Gulch. Gregane had promised an answer the following day, and then sent out scouts to check the terrain. It would be at least a day or two before he heard back from them, and the knight found his patience wearing thin as the night waned.

"I'd have preferred it if we had chosen the location," Nicholls admitted. "But assuming Arthur holds to his word, we couldn't have hoped for better ground to fight. It'd take months to starve him out of his caves, if at all given how many damn hidden paths and vaults he's dug into it."

Gregane nodded. When he'd marched out, granted command by Lord Sebastian, he'd expected to be heading toward a lengthy siege. With his five thousand men, a tenth of them mounted cavalry, he'd figured Arthur would use his castle to make up for his vastly inferior numbers. Such a plan, while sure to be an eventual victory for Gregane, posed far greater danger than open combat. The plain folk were, without a doubt, supporting and aiding Arthur. The longer the brothers' conflict lasted, the worse it'd get for Sebastian.

"If it comes down to the Green Gulch, a potential siege, or a fight at a river crossing, I'll take the flat ground," said Gregane.

Nicholls rolled up the map and stored it in a chest of Gregane's things.

"What of the scouts?" he asked.

"Learn what we can from them, but unless they discover battlements and trenches already built, we'll not break our word."

"Will Arthur renege? This could be a ploy."

Gregane shook his head.

"I've served the Hemman family since long before Arthos's death. I know Arthur. He's honorable, and will do what he thinks is right. He would never renege upon an agreed battle."

"What of his rebellion against Sebastian? I assume he thinks it is right, too?"

Gregane sighed, and he yanked his sword free and gestured for Nicholls to leave.

"Careful with your thoughts," he said. "That road leads to danger. We serve the lord of the North, and right now, that rightful lord is Sebastian Hemman. All else matters not."

"Of course," Nicholls said, saluting. When he was gone, Gregane scowled. His anger toward Nicholls was misplaced, and he knew it. The younger knight had only voiced a gnawing doubt that he himself had been trying to ignore. Arthur, the older brother, was the one who should have ruled, if not for forsaking his claim. Arthur, the one who ruled all aspects of his life with honor, and patience ...

He slammed his fist atop the table, banishing such treasonous thoughts. Sebastian was lord. That was that. Gregane couldn't toss a bag of coins to beggars, then demand it back the following year. It was foolish, and neither could Arthur try for similar. Such threats to the North's stability needed to be ended, and quickly. His duty wasn't to like it, only do it. Come battle, he would defeat Arthur, and bring him bound to the Yellow Castle for his lord to decree his fate.

A cold wind blew, and he shivered. The tent flap rustled, and he turned thinking it only the wind. Instead, a man in black robes stood before him, his pale face smiling and his eyes alive with fire. Gregane reached for his sword, but stopped when the man said a single word.

"Halt."

Despite his struggle, Gregane could not move. It was as if a hundred invisible chains had latched to his body. He stared at the intruder, feeling anger and panic swelling in his chest. His heart pounded, the sound thunderous in his ears.

"I mean you no harm," said the man in black. "And I stop you not out of fear or malice, but to prevent you from doing something you might regret. If you remain calm, I will release you."

Unsure how to answer, Gregane stared at the man and did his best to show that he was under control. Apparently it worked, for the intruder waved his hand, and the chains were gone.

"Who are you?" he asked, crossing his arms to fight against the impulse to draw his blade.

"I am Velixar, voice of the Lion, prophet to our glorious god Karak. I come offering counsel, and my aid."

"I have enough men whispering in my ears."

"Yes, but I offer no whispers, and most important of all, my voice speaks truth."

Gregane swallowed. Truth, he thought. He highly doubted it. Still, if this was a holy man of Karak, he had to tread carefully. Sebastian's loyalty to their deity was well known throughout the North.

"Then tell me what you wish to say, and I will take it into consideration."

"Consideration?" Velixar chuckled, though Gregane could not begin to guess the reason for his amusement. "When men with wisdom speak, you should listen, and obey, my dear knight. Not pretend. Not take it into consideration."

Gregane found himself entranced by the prophet's face. At first he'd thought he imagined it, but he realized the man's features were slowly shifting, as if his face were a liquid in constant, miniscule motion. His blood ran cold as he wondered just what really lay behind that mask.

"As you say," Gregane said, trying to play it safe. "Then speak, and I will listen."

"Much better. I have seen many battles, Sir ...?"

"Gregane."

"Sir Gregane. I've seen many, and started more. I know the minds of men, the simple strategies they employ. Let me stay at your side, and I will help you crush Arthur's rebellion. The North's worship of Karak must not be disrupted in any way."

Gregane thought of that priest standing beside him come the battle, and he knew any orders he gave would not be suggestions. Once more he felt another clawing at the prestige that was to be rightfully his. And staring into those red eyes, he knew within lurked a man who would laugh at the very notion of honorable combat.

"We go to meet Arthur's men," he said. "We have agreed to a place, and will arrive within a few day's march. Would you accompany us, or wait for our arrival?"

It was a gamble, he knew, but he had a feeling such a man would not casually walk among the living. His very presence seemed counter to daylight.

"I will await you there," the priest said, his smile growing. "Show me where."

Gregane knelt before his chest, opened it, and pulled out his map. Carefully he unrolled it upon the lone table of his tent, placing weights on all four corners to keep it open. With every bit of his self control, he willed himself to believe with absolute certainty the lie he spoke.

"Here," he said, pointing to a place labeled Deer Valley, several miles east of the Green Gulch.

"A valley?" Velixar asked.

"We will leave them nowhere to run, and our horsemen will run rampant through their lines."

The prophet nodded in approval.

"My faithful and I will await you there, my good knight. Your cooperation will never be forgotten, I promise."

The promise felt just as much threat, but Gregane kept his face composed, the rigid gaze of a commander. Velixar stepped out from the tent. Once he was gone, Gregane collapsed to his knees, tore off his armor, and called out for one of his servants to bring him a very, very full pitcher of wine.

14

Jerico rode into Lord Arthur's camp with his head held high, as beside him Kaide busily counted and made estimations. Finding the army had taken little questioning, considering every farmer and trader seemed to know of its location. As they neared, they'd encountered villages Arthur's men had passed through, accepting gifts of food and supplies. From there, they'd found the army with ease. Kaide's group had been stopped at the outer edges of the camp, but the guards were aware of their coming, and let them pass.

"I hate the way they look at us," Bellok said, guiding his horse between Jerico and Kaide. "Like filthy rabble."

"Are you saying we're not?" Kaide said, but he didn't smile at his own joke, instead too busy glancing about at the tents.

"Nervous to meet Arthur again?" Bellok asked.

"Or have your men embarrass you?" Jerico added, glancing back to the farmers, thieves, and bandits that formed their diminutive group. Most seemed intimidated by the armored soldiers that watched them trot toward the center of the camp, marked by Arthur's enormous tent atop a cluster of hills.

"No," Kaide said, frowning. "I count only a thousand, maybe fifteen-hundred. I hoped for more."

"More might come," Bellok said, but he sounded like he doubted it.

At the commander's tent, they halted and dismounted. A soldier guarding the entrance motioned to a field in the far distance.

"We've prepared a place for your ... group," said the man.

"That's a damn long walk," Kaide said.

"We have some food to spare, and the land is flat. Do you have a problem?"

Jerico and Kaide exchanged looks.

"So be it," Kaide said. "Bellok, spread the order, then join us inside."

As they went to enter, the guard refused to move. Instead he pointed to the mace, shield, and dirks the two wore.

"Your weapons," he said.

Another look between them.

"No," they said in unison.

The guard didn't seem flustered in the slightest.

"Surrender, or no audience."

The tent flap opened, and Lord Arthur stepped out long enough to gesture them inside, as well as whisper a word to the guard. The guard shot them an annoyed glare, but held his tongue. A fire built in the center of the tent made the interior feel warm and welcoming, the smoke escaping through a hole in the very top where the poles came together. A table was on one side, adorned with maps and sheets of parchment detailing numbers and supplies. On the other side was Arthur's bed. The lord walked over to the table and sat in the only chair.

"I must thank you," Arthur said, leaning back. "Given how quickly I prepared my forces, I feared I would have no choice but to take from the villagers we passed to keep my men fed. Instead, I find myself given more than my fattest soldier can eat. Never did I think the hearts of the people had abandoned my brother so."

"The hearts of most can be bought with coin," Kaide said. "And I've spent every day since Ashvale buying hearts using Sebastian's own gold."

Arthur let out a bitter chuckle.

"I see. I pray you never turn on me, Kaide. It could be disastrous for us both."

"When will your entire force be assembled?" Jerico asked, trying to bring the conversation to the tasks at hand.

"When? It already is, paladin. Are you disappointed?"

Jerico was unsure of what to say, so Kaide said it for him.

"Yes. We are. What challenge will we be to Sebastian's men with only, what, a thousand?"

"Fourteen hundred, not counting retainers, squires, and the women lurking about waiting for night to fall. I summoned those loyal to me to fight, and now you act disappointed? I'd hoped the legendary bandit would make up for that. How many men did you bring me?"

Kaide's face remained passive as stone.

"Three hundred."

"Three hundred?" The lord laughed. "Surely the might of the people rises up against my brother. Three hundred, armed with what? Pitchforks? Knives?"

"Enough," Jerico said. "What is it you plan to do, Arthur?"

The lord gestured to the map, and the two looked over it. Its location marked with an embedded dagger, they saw his proposed site for a battle.

"Green Gulch?" Kaide asked.

"Sir Gregane has already sent a rider agreeing to the place. We'll meet at midday, and fight each other on an honest field of battle."

Kaide looked ready to fall over.

"*Honest* field of battle? We're going to be outnumbered, and you want to march south into a scattered forest full of level ground and fight an honest battle? Would you throw this war away so easily?"

"Men fight wars, Kaide. A skilled, proud man fighting a worthy cause can defeat ten sworn to something they do not believe. How many men have you killed with just your few?"

"With surprise. With stealth. Abandon the designated spot, and march with all haste toward the cities. Take Murkland. Take Valewood. With them in your control, Sebastian will have to come running, and by then, we might already have a second army headed for his castle!"

Arthur waved him off.

"You appealed to my honor to start this war, now ask me to cast it off when you find it inconvenient? A victory here means the end of our conflict, with no villages burned, no lives lost other than fighting men sworn to such a fate. Now enough of this. You have your three hundred. What is it you would like to do with them? I can find a place among my ranks, not the front lines, of course ..."

They heard commotion from outside, and then Bellok entered, adjusting his robes.

"It'll do," he said to Kaide, referring to the encampment. He turned to Lord Arthur. "Oh, and the Irons twins might have knocked one of your soldiers unconscious. Well, several of your soldiers. No one died, I promise."

Arthur's eyes widened.

"May I ask the reason?"

Bellok bit his lip and glanced at Kaide.

"I'd suggest not. Suffice to say, your men will not speak ill of those two again, nor their mothers, nor the animals they ride on."

Arthur rubbed his eyes and looked ready to dismiss them all.

"My men," Kaide said, bringing his attention back to the map. "I have a plan for them, though it might insult your honorable tendencies. Where will you set up your lines?"

Arthur gestured to a small white space.

"There runs a gap of nearly half a mile between the trees. My men will be stationed along the tree line. That should keep Sebastian's mounted knights from running us over."

Kaide looked at it, and gestured for Bellok to do the same. The wizard ran a hand through his white hair, and then nodded in approval.

"It'll work," he said.

"What will?" asked Arthur.

"I think it best you not know," Kaide said. "I have my tricks, just as you have your noble honor. Until we reach the Gulch, we'll march with you, but continue on when you begin setting up lines."

Arthur looked none too pleased with this, but he did not argue.

"Sir Gregane is leading Sebastian's forces," he said. "He's a good man, and knows how to fight. Whatever you do, prepare for it to not work as you expect. Other than that, from where we believe them camped, we'll have about a half-day's preparation before he arrives. Can you do what you hope to do in such short time?"

"I could do it in less," Bellok said, shooting the lord a grin.

"Just who are you, again?" Arthur asked.

"The card I have hidden up my sleeve," Kaide said, bowing low. "Now by your leave, I'd like to return to my men."

"Go." He waved them on, but when he saw Jerico about to leave, he stopped him.

"Yes, milord?" Jerico asked.

"I heard plenty of opinions, but none from you. What say you to all this?"

"I don't know Kaide's plan. He's hidden it from even me. As to where you battle, the advantages are as you say, and will be better if you can dig even a single trench beforehand. How many men do you expect to fight?"

"Four to five thousand."

The two stood there a moment in the quiet, and then Arthur began to chuckle.

"I march men to their deaths, all for a cause I cannot win. That's the truth of this, isn't it?"

Jerico shrugged.

"If that is so, then why do you continue?"

Arthur sat in his chair and leaned back, eyeing the paladin.

"I looked into you, Jerico, to see what I could find. The Citadel ... there's a story spreading, though how it fell no one seems to agree. Your paladin friends are vanishing, and some whispers even say they are gone completely. Yet here you are, still fighting. Why is that?"

Jerico shrugged.

"It's the right thing to do."

"Aye," Arthur said, and for once he smiled. "It is. After hiding in caves for years, it feels good to stand tall and do just that. I dare say, it is about damn time. Will you fight at my side, or will you join Kaide's dogs lurking at the edges?"

"I don't even know what Kaide is doing. Until I do, I must stay with him. I think he'll need my help more than you will. In fact, I'm certain of it. I did help train his men, after all."

Arthur laughed.

"You did? How did that go?"

"I lasted a day before I wanted to break my vows to Ashhur involving decency and murder."

Arthur stood, and he clasped Jerico's hand and shook it.

"Stand tall, and fight bravely," he said. "Consider me honored to have known you, and have you fight against my brother, wherever you may be."

Jerico smiled, and he did his best to push away all thoughts of the coming battle.

"Ashhur be with you," he said, leaving the tent to speak with Kaide and find out just what chaos he had in mind.

❈

Darius and Velixar camped alone several miles from Deer Valley. Velixar never slept, but he often vanished for long periods of prayer. It was then Darius would sleep. Rarely did he feel rested come morning. Nightmares haunted him, always of the Abyss. He felt its heat beneath his skin. In the darkness, he saw what would be his fate, his torture and release upon accepting his rightful place in the eyes of his god. With fire and flame he would cleanse the sin from the wretched.

But in his dreams he suffered with the sufferers, despite everything Velixar insisted.

Yet those dreams were still better than having Velixar's burning eyes upon him, or to hear his cold words whispering promises and assurances. He wanted rest, needed it badly, but this time, as the stars rose, the prophet did not leave for prayer.

"Will you need a fire?" he asked as the two sat in the center of their modest camp. Darius nodded. Winter was fast approaching, the last remnants of autumn's warmth in retreat. A fire sprang forth between them with a wave of Velixar's hand, and Darius leaned closer to it, his arms hunched and his head low.

"You know what must be done," Velixar said, watching him from beneath his hood. "Come tomorrow, it will all end. The last consequence of your failure will be faced. Amid Arthur's army lurks the paladin. I am sure of it. No mere soldier will bring him down. That honor must be yours. What will you do when you meet him in battle?"

Darius thought of the man he'd always considered his friend, however strained their friendship had been because of their opposed deities. What would he do?

"It doesn't matter," he said, refusing to look Velixar in the eye. "I will do what Karak asks of me."

"Karak's will has often proved elusive to you. I would have an answer, paladin."

Darius looked up, and he felt a weight upon his heart as he spoke.

"I will kill him. I will cut his head from his shoulders, and hold it high for all Dezrel to see. My faith is to Karak, my god, above all others. Let him go to Ashhur, or Karak, or wherever his soul shall spend eternity."

A smile spread across Velixar's ever-changing face.

"You have learned much, Darius, enough that I would consider you both pupil and friend. I know your heart is still troubled. Do not think me blind to your struggles. But freedom comes soon. Bear no guilt for what must be done. Think not of him as your friend, nor as an enemy. He is an obstacle in your path, blocking the narrow road. In this, you must know what Karak has called for. You cannot doubt my words. Since your childhood, Karak has demanded this of you, that you let nothing stand in the way of your faith. Not death, not life, not love, not weakness, and not pride. Faith, Darius. You have it, stronger than most alive, and that is why I offer you a gift, if you would accept it."

Darius felt a shiver travel up his spine, and he tried to blame it on the weather.

"What is your gift?" he asked.

"Let me see the mark on your hand."

Darius pulled back his sleeve and held out his sword hand. The skin remained black as charcoal, and looked as if it had been recently charred. It caused him no pain, other than a constant remembrance of his doubt and weakness back in Durham. Velixar put his own hands atop it, his touch like ice.

"Karak marked you, for you went to him seeking your fate if you spared Jerico's life," Velixar said. "Now you have seen it, and lived it, all the while bearing Karak's shame. You doubted his will. You tried to bring mercy to an enemy that deserves only annihilation. Tell me once more the fate you saw."

"I would fall at his feet," Darius said, and he felt tears building in his eyes. "I'd be beaten, bloodied, and like a dog I would beg for death."

"I free you from that fate," Velixar said. "I free you from Karak's mark. Your faith has returned, and it will grow stronger than ever. Know Karak's love has come into you. Know his presence, in his greatest way."

Velixar's hands shimmered violently.

Everywhere the mark touched flared with pain, as if Darius had plunged his hand into fire. His arm shook. His stomach twisted, but he had not eaten in a day, and he had nothing to expel. A vision came over him, shocking with its strength and power. He saw himself, and at first he thought it taking place in the Abyss given the fire surrounding them, but then he saw grass and trees. Bodies lay about, cut down by blades

On his knees, his mace lost, his shield broken, knelt Jerico.

One last chance, he heard himself say. *Yield to Karak, or face his judgment.*

Jerico stared at him, his face full of anguish and sorrow. He said nothing, only shook his head. Darius felt himself dip into the body of the vision, becoming one with it. Sensations nearly overwhelmed him; the heat of the fire, the ache of his muscles from the fight, and the taste of blood on his tongue. Most of all, though, he felt pure, total exhilaration.

He lifted his sword, wreathed with black flame so thick it hid the blade completely. It felt light as air in his hands. His mark, which had marred his skin, was gone. Jerico looked to the blade, then closed his eyes.

Karak's judgment, Darius heard, though he knew not who said it. *It comes for all.*

He swung the sword. As it connected with Jerico's neck, the vision shattered, and he felt himself returning to his true body. He lay on his back in the grass, shivering from the cold. To his left, the fire had dwindled down to nothing. Velixar stood over the ashes, and even he looked shaken.

"Such glory," he said, his voice soft. "Such honor. Your mark is gone, Darius, and your fate now your own. Show faith to Karak, and you will achieve all you have seen. Fail, doubt, and you will break before Jerico. Two destinies, both yours to decide. Either Jerico falls, or you fall before him. I have faith in you to make the right choice, to wield the power meant to be yours. Karak's strength embodies you. Stand, Darius. Lift your blade."

Darius did, and though he felt unsteady on his feet, he could not deny how much lighter his armor felt. When he lifted his sword, it was with a single hand instead of two. At his touch, fire consumed it, dark and deep. The metal of the blade was visible, but only just.

"My choice," Darius said.

"It always has been."

Darius looked to Velixar.

"Then I will live, and bring Order to a world that sorely needs it."

Velixar's smile was ear to ear.

"As it should be," he said. "Karak be praised. You have truly returned to the fold."

Darius sheathed his sword, closed his eyes, and gave his first ever prayer to Ashhur. He asked him to keep his champion from partaking in the battle. Otherwise, his mind was decided. His fate was chosen.

Should they meet, Jerico would die.

15

"You're grumpier than normal," Jerico said as Bellok shouted orders at every nearby person, whether they deserved it or not.

"The whole damn night," the wizard said, rubbing his eyes. "Ever tried swinging your mace for eight hours straight? I did that with my head. Grumpy doesn't begin to describe how I feel. The next person who yells next to my ear gets turned into a jumping toad."

They walked amid the bustle of the camp, preparing to move out. Arthur had sent them a rider, alerting them to Gregane's location. Come the late afternoon, the battle would begin.

"Are we ready?" Jerico asked, tightening his armor. "I still don't know our plan."

"Better you don't. It's not going to work."

"This the grumpiness talking?"

"Common sense. Now where's that blasted little brat, Kaide?"

Jerico pointed toward the top of a hill.

"Giving his best speech to the men."

Bellok rubbed his temples with his fingers.

"I don't have time for speeches. Let me just show you, then."

The paladin followed him to the wizard's tent. Inside was a chest, its lid closed. Before Jerico even took a step inside, Bellok whirled on him, jamming a finger against his breastplate.

"Whatever you do," he said, "not even if Ashhur himself commanded it, not even if you thought your very life depended on it, do not bump that chest. Understood?"

Jerico stammered, his jaw working up and down as if it might somehow figure out a correct response.

"Um ... understood?"

Bellok eyed him, clearly not believing, but then turned to the chest and carefully opened the lid. Jerico leaned forward, curious to see what the fuss was about.

"Rocks?" he said. "I must confess, Bellok, I expected something a little more ... impressive?"

The look the wizard gave him made him feel like a child, and he started to blush.

"Rocks," Bellok said, his voice flat. "I spent all night casting spells, turning these into our one slim hope of victory, and you come in and call them unimpressive rocks? Do you think me a loon that guards a few plain stones like they were Karak's balls?"

"But I—"

"Did you not think for even a moment they might be hidden, or of a magical nature? A wizard's stash of artifacts, after all, might just be magical."

"But—"

"And did it not once ever occur to you," Bellok said, now nearly roaring while jamming his finger an inch away from Jerico's nose, "that just maybe, *maybe*, there is an inherent deception involved in the creation of certain artifacts, or that the plain might be infused with the magical, just like your miniscule little brain somehow manages to swing a giant mace to smash other miniscule little brains?"

Jerico stared at him, torn between laughing and running in terror. He started to speak, stopped, watched Bellok narrow his eyes as if anticipating another stupid comment, and then spoke.

"I just—"

"Forget it. Would you like to see what they do?"

Jerico sighed.

"Yes."

Bellok knelt by the chest and delicately picked up one of the stones. They were about the size of his palm, and smooth on all sides. He gestured for Jerico to follow, and then left the tent with the chest lid still open. Jerico glanced within, saw about twenty more of the stones, and then hurried after.

"Wands and staves are beyond anything Kaide's men might use," Bellok said as he led them away from the camp. "But I think even these are within their skills."

They stopped at the stump of a tree, cut down the night before for firewood.

"Take off your gauntlet," Bellok said.

"Why?"

"Because I don't want you to die from too rough of a touch. Gods, how Ashhur puts up with you is beyond me."

Biting his tongue, Jerico removed his gauntlets and set them aside. Accepting the stone with his bare hand, he was immediately struck by how warm it was to the touch. Bellok pointed to the stump.

"Throw it."

Jerico wound up and hurled the stone, and only as it left his hand did he realize Bellok had retreated a significant distance. The stone struck the stump, and instead of bouncing off like it should have, it broke into pieces. With a bright flash, the pieces burst into flame. The fire spread rapidly, as if the surrounding area were bathed in oil. Jerico let out a shout at the sudden heat, and he jumped backward. Nearly stumbling, he caught himself, then glared at Bellok's far too pleased expression.

"Rocks," the wizard said with a smug grin. "Still unimpressed?"

"Far from it," Jerico said, looking back. The stump was already black, the fire spreading to the dead grass nearby. The paladin feared a wildfire, but then the wizard raised his hands and whispered words of power. The fire lessened, and then died.

"These will certainly kill a man," Jerico said, grabbing his gauntlets. "The surprise will be huge."

Bellok scoffed.

"I would not have them used for something so brutish and simple. I show you a brilliant weapon, and all you can think of is to throw it at the enemy like a child? Think, paladin. Remember the terrain we are to fight on, and where Arthur plans to hold his defense."

Jerico paused, and then it clicked into place.

"The forest," he said. Bellok grinned.

"We'll surround them with fire, leave Sebastian's men with nowhere to run. With these stones, they'll find themselves in the midst of an inferno before they even smell a whiff of smoke. Burning them alive may not be honorable, but Sebastian cast aside honor long ago."

Jerico bit his lower lip in thought. It could work, though he doubted it would be as simple as the wizard hoped. Of course, there was one other major flaw.

"Promise me one thing," he said.

"What's that?"

"Adam and Griff don't get to carry one."

Bellok finally laughed.

"Perhaps there is some shred of intelligence hidden under that skull of yours."

"Thanks," Jerico muttered, following him back to camp.

Once there, the paladin found Kaide grabbing a drink of wine for his parched throat.

"How'd it go?" Jerico asked.

"Were you not there to listen?"

"Afraid not. Was getting lectured by the wizard."

Kaide shrugged.

"I did my best. We'll have surprise on our side. Won't be able to ride our horses, though. Saddles aren't right for it, and neither riders nor horses are trained. We'll fight on foot, with knives, clubs, and a few stolen swords. To think this is what I wanted. Should Sebastian turn on us with any real amount of numbers, our line will break like water."

"Not all of it," Jerico said, lifting his shield so its light shone across Kaide's face. "I will be at your side. Your line will not break, so long as we stand."

Kaide smiled, and it lit his handsome face. It was the first true smile Jerico had seen from him.

"As you say, we'll make it be. Thank you, Jerico."

"My pleasure. Just don't run on me. I'd hate for you to miss your own victory."

Sir Gregane stared across the open field to the distant forest on the other side of the half-mile gap.

"A fair place for a battle," Nicholls said, looking at the smooth terrain. "Arthur chose well."

"They were here before us," Gregane said as he glanced at his vanguard. "We must act carefully. There may be hidden ditches to break our horses' legs, or tripwire laced between the trees."

"All that seems a bit low for one such as Arthur."

Gregane frowned.

"Arthur consorts with brigands and murderers. We cannot assume he has gone unchanged."

He stared at the field, confident no ambushes lurked there. The grass was too short to conceal a man, and there were no hills tall enough to hide behind. He saw faint whiffs of smoke from the forest, and even at their distance, he could tell the entire army waited within.

"Fighting amid trees," he muttered. "We'll need to draw them out."

"A minor advantage," Nicholls argued.

"Not if they flee. But first, let's see if Arthur is willing to submit before any blood is shed."

Gregane's vanguard, twenty knights and their mounts, all fully armored, rode with multiple banners waving the sigil of the Yellow Rose. From the forest Arthur rode out to meet them, with only five at his side. They too wore armor, and it shone in the afternoon light. When they were within a hundred yards, Gregane motioned for his vanguard to halt, and then he rode forward alone, as did Arthur.

"Greetings, Sir Gregane," Arthur said, lifting the visor of his helmet. "Have you come to aid my rightful return as lord of the Yellow Rose?"

"You forfeited that claim," Gregane said. "Please, Arthur, I ask you to throw down your sword and go home. You can see our numbers. There is no hope for you here, only death."

"Are those your terms?" Arthur asked. "Disarm myself, and run like a frightened child to cower and hide for the next assassin to come? I will not live my life frightened of my drink and distrusting every shadow of my room. Sebastian tried to take my life. He failed. I will come for his, and I will succeed."

Gregane shook his head.

"Very well. I have one last offer, this from Sebastian himself. Dismiss your army, and announce to the people of the North that Sebastian is still lord of the Yellow Rose. In return, milord will bear no grudge against you, ensure no assassins ever dare strike at you, and allow you the freedom to leave your Castle of Caves without fear. What say you?"

Arthur grinned, and the wolfish gleam in his eye told Gregane the answer before the lord ever spoke.

"His promises are nothing. One last chance, Gregane. The men will listen to you. Join my side. I am the eldest son, and I have come for my birthright."

Sir Gregane saluted, even as he felt sadness pang in his heart.

"Ready your men," he said. "It comes to bloodshed, then."

Arthur saluted in return.

"I pray we do not meet in battle," he said. "For no matter the victor, I will always offer my hand to you in friendship, should you ever choose to accept it."

They rode back to their escorts.

"Well?" Nicholls asked.

"Prepare the archers," Gregane said. "I want the whole damn woods buried with arrows."

Nicholls shouted the order, and then the army began marching. As expected, Arthur vanished into the forest behind the many trunks and naked branches. No troops came out to meet them as they marched. It looked like they wished to fight amid the trees, but Gregane had no intention of doing so.

Once within two hundred yards, Gregane called a halt. Archers rushed to the front, forming three lines of a hundred each. Sir Gregane lifted his arm, and he looked through the trees at the line of soldiers. Somewhere in there, an honorable lord would die. Such a shame.

"Let loose," he said.

Volley after volley sailed into the air, and in the silence following the twang of bowstrings, Gregane sighed.

The arrows hit the forest like rain. Even from their distance, Gregane could hear the sounds of pierced trunks, snapped shafts, and the screams of the wounded. Of all, it was the third that was the least. Frowning, he ordered another volley. Again the arrows fell, and Gregane struggled to see. The trees were too much cover, from what he could tell, and the men on the front lines bore heavy shields.

"What now?" Nicholls asked.

"Arrows are replaced easier than men," Gregane said. "Empty every quiver."

The twang of the bowstrings became a discordant chorus, the archers letting loose as fast as they were capable. Gregane did not even watch, instead turning to his troops and planning strategy. His knights would lose most advantages navigating their horses through the trees. If only he could draw Arthur's men out somehow, and then send his knights crashing through their sides ...

"Advance slowly," Gregane said. "Tight formations, no charge. Let us see how disciplined our enemy is. And watch for traps."

The archers fell to the back, and then the squads of footmen began their approach. Only a third were equipped with shields, and they would be the ones on the frontlines. The rest carried heavy swords and axes, the killing men that would break through once the initial clash was done. Gregane stayed back with his knights, watching for the perfect moment to send them crashing in.

The yards between them shrank, and Gregane found himself holding his breath waiting for the collision of bodies, the communal yell of a charge. It did not come, for behind him he heard the sound of an inferno unleashed.

"What in Karak's name is that?" Nicholls shouted. Gregane spun his horse, and he felt his heart hammer in his chest at the sight.

The woods behind them were ablaze. Not just burning, not just smoking, but full ablaze, every tree consumed, every inch of the sky blotted out above it. As trees collapsed and branches fell, the grassland caught.

"The wind," Gregane said, fighting off panic.

"It is with us," Nicholls said, but he didn't sound convinced. "The fire will not catch us. It'll burn west instead."

At such a sight, it was hard to believe. Swearing, he looked back to the fight. Most were unaware of the inferno, no doubt focused on the battle. His squads had reached the forest, which remained at a standstill. Shields locked against shields. Those with the longer swords stabbed over, and Gregane knew he was killing just as many, if not more, than Arthur. But that fire ...

He glanced back, and this time saw a disturbing sight. Running low to the ground were several hundred men, racing ahead of the fire. Amid the smoke they were difficult to spot, but luck had been with him, a heavy gust pushing the smoke away so he might see. Cursing, he took stock of the new threat.

"It must be the bandits," he said.

Nicholls turned, for a moment confused. Following Gregane's point, he saw the group and frowned.

"I see no heavy armor," he said. "I think you're right. What do we do?"

The fight was not yet theirs, but they could not afford to be pressed from two directions, no matter how weak that second force might be. It seemed overkill to use his knights, but the bandits were on open ground.

"Take half," he told Nicholls. "Wipe them out quickly, then return."

"Right," said the knight, drawing his sword. Calling out orders, he trotted ahead, two hundred and fifty men riding behind. Gregane turned his attention back to the forest, trusting his fellow knight to deal with the distraction. At first he smiled, for Arthur's line had clearly broken, but then he saw his men remained in tight formations just within the tree line. They certainly didn't look like an army giving chase.

"Find out what's going on," he told one of his riders. The man shot off, rode a half-circle behind the lines, and then returned.

"They built themselves a ditch," said the rider. "Fell back, and now are killing any trying to climb across."

Sir Gregane swore, then spurred his horse onward.

"To me!" he cried, and several nearby took up his cry to ensure he was heard over the chaos of the battle. "To me, fall back!"

His men did as they were told, and Gregane clenched his teeth as Arthur's men launched an assault. Gregane's footmen, torn between standing their ground and retreating as ordered, suffered terrible casualties before reforming their lines outside the trees. Those that chased turned back, vanishing into the forest. Gregane rode past his lines, estimating numbers. Hundreds dead already, if not a thousand. Still, he outnumbered Arthur, but such brutal losses ...

"Get the archers," he told his vanguard. "I want them shoving every last body into the ditch. We'll charge across the dead, both theirs and ours. Rob, Ash, ride to either side and find out just how far that ditch goes. I want them flanked come our next charge."

The two knights saluted and obeyed. As the archers rushed forward, and his men reset their lines, he glanced back to see how long until Nicholls returned. Instead, his mouth fell agape at the sight. The fire had spread, ignoring the wind as if it were possessed. Already a quarter mile of grassland burned. Gregane swore at whatever sorcery had to be involved. A second fire appeared to have erupted at the feet of his charging knights. Every which way he saw horses sprinting, some with riders, some without. The leather of their saddles, and sometimes their very bodies, burned. Those that had survived appeared locked in combat, though he was too far to know how that went. Amidst all this strangeness was a strong blue light. No matter where his knights rode, no matter who struck at it, the light never faded, never broke.

"Sir," said Rob, returning from his side. "It goes on for at a tenth mile, though most of it appears unguarded."

"They'll shift over should they see us moving," Gregane said, but he eyed the stretch of forest with a thought. "We have numbers, though. They can't cover it all."

Ash returned, the young knight telling of a similar setup. It seemed in what time they had, Arthur had done nothing but build the enormous ditch, hoping to use it as a killing ground. With the trees to hide them from the arrows that could break them, the strategy was simple but sound.

"Pull back two squads," Gregane said. "Send one to each side. March until you see no one guarding the ditch, then wait for my signal."

"Yes, sir," said the two knights before riding off to do as they were told. Gregane watched the forest a while longer, until it was clear little combat occurred. Steadily the archers grabbed bodies, and guarded by his shielded footmen, hurled them into the ditch. Outnumbered, and with their own ditch between them, Arthur's men couldn't dare charge. Body by body, their only defense vanished, and from three sides Gregane would strike.

Assuming the fire didn't come to consume them all. Another glance back showed it getting closer, though it'd still take an hour to reach them. He shuddered to think how quick it might have spread if the wind had been toward them instead. As for his knights, he found himself stunned at how few their numbers had become. More stunning was how they turned and bolted in retreat. Anger grew in his chest, and when Nicholls came leading, Gregane let out his fury.

"Armorless bandits?" he roared. "My best-trained, defeated by mere peasants with clubs?"

"They hurled fire like sorcerers," Nicholls said, refusing to lower his head or show weakness at the outburst. "And armorless or not, they wielded heavy weaponry, and struck at our horses. The fire alone spooked them, and they had a wizard whose very words sent our mounts running at random. We could not control them."

"The blue light," Gregane said, trying to calm down. "What of that?"

"Shield of a paladin," Nicholls said. "A skilled man. He stands like a mountain, and nothing moves him. I saw Oren ram his horse straight into that shield, and it was the horse that fell."

Gregane was stunned. He looked about, counting, and couldn't believe it.

"A hundred dead?"

"Thirty to the fire," Nicholls said. "The rest to the brigands. We killed as many as we lost, but know I mean it when I say that paladin cannot link up with the rest of Arthur's men, or we will all suffer."

Gregane looked to the forest, suddenly fearful of a strange sorcerer and a holy warrior of Ashhur both guarding the line. If they could ward off mounted knights in open field, what could they do in such close combat?

"You say the wizard could disturb the horses?" he asked.

"He did. They turned and startled every which way. No rider can fight like that."

"Then don't ride. All of you, dismount. If my own vanguard cannot defeat them, we are not worthy to call ourselves knights. Now go! Come back with that paladin's head, or not at all."

Nicholls saluted, but Gregane could see the hesitation in his eyes. Damn fool. They would outnumber them near two to one. How could they lose? Only the fire posed a threat, a fire that continued toward them like a crawling monster. Struggling to keep his patience, he once more turned his attention to the forest. Alone, he marched toward his troops, drawing his sword. Enough of giving commands. Soon the ditch would be full, and both Ash and Rob would have their hundred men in position. It wouldn't matter how many casualties he suffered in the long run. Once Arthur fell, the North would remain Sebastian's, now and forever.

Gregane could only hope that such an honor, of killing Lord Arthur, would belong to him, and him alone.

16

Valessa waited with Mallak in the lower portion of Deer Valley. Ever since waking that morning, and seeing nothing but distant campfires miles away, she'd had a nagging fear they'd been betrayed. The only question was by whom.

"Velixar would never lie," Mallak said when she voiced her fears. "Not to us. Not to anyone. If someone lied, then it was to him. Let us be patient, and see what becomes of this."

Valessa spent the time sharpening her daggers and imagining them plunging into Arthur Hemman's eyes for what he'd done to Claire. Mallak cooked their morning meal, and she ate, tasting nothing of the nuts and salted pork slivers. The sun rose, and still they heard no sound of marching feet, saw no sign of approaching armies. Time crawled along, until at last Velixar and Darius appeared in the distance, walking into the valley by themselves.

"No one is here," Velixar said the moment they were within earshot.

"As it seems," said Mallak. "But this is where the armies were to meet, didn't Sir Gregane say?"

Valessa watched Velixar's ever-changing face harden into a visage of smoldering anger.

"He plays a dangerous game if he thinks to interfere with Karak's doings."

"Might they be delayed somehow?" Valessa asked. Already she knew the answer, but it amused her to see the prophet flustered so. In the daylight, he was far from the intimidating specter he was at night. His skin seemed paler, his bones visible through his stretched skin. Even the fire in his eyes was but a dull red glow.

"Be silent," he said, closing his eyes and lifting his hands. "I will find them."

They waited as the prophet cast his spell. Valessa used the time to steal a glance at Darius. She noticed the mark on his hand was gone and felt her stomach tighten at that. Such a sure sign of Karak's forgiveness was hard to dispute, crushing her hopes for a chance to take his life. It was because of him Claire had died, a direct result of his lapse in faith. Karak might welcome the return of the faithful, but Valessa was not her deity. She wanted blood. Darius himself looked tired, still drained and lifeless as he had been when she first saw him at Velixar's side.

Champion of Karak, she thought. Such a joke.

"The fool," Velixar said, suddenly opening his eyes. "They are in the Gulch, many miles away."

"We'll not make it in time," Valessa said. "We'll have to trust Sebastian's men to achieve victory."

Velixar looked at her as if she were a child.

"The shadows are my doorways," he said. "We will arrive, though not as fast as if at night. Come with me, all of you."

Velixar hurried them toward the closest copse of trees near the edge of the valley. On their way, they saw smoke rise to the west, first thin, then shockingly heavy.

"Have they set the entire gulch aflame?" Valessa wondered, but none had an answer for her.

At the trees, Velixar circled about, stepping into their shade.

"Weak," he said. "But enough."

Casting a spell, he tore a swirling portal into existence, then beckoned for them to enter. Darius went first, followed by Mallak. Valessa smiled at Velixar, then blew him a kiss before stepping through. Her stomach immediately twisted, and she nearly vomited upon stepping out. She felt herself having crossed a great distance, but it was something she could not fully understand, and her whole body revolted against the sensation. They were amid a heavy cluster of trees packed so dense they provided shade from the sun despite their lack of leaves.

"How many times?" Valessa asked, all her mocking humor gone because of the unsettling method of travel.

"Many," Velixar said, his voice cold. "The sun will make this travel difficult, but I will do what I can. Arthur must lose, and Jerico must be slain by Darius. If I am denied this ..."

He closed his eyes and began casting again. Taking in a breath, Valessa noticed how focused the prophet seemed, how weak he appeared in the daylight. She felt her dagger in her hand, and looked to Darius, whose lifeless eyes stared into a world far from their own.

"Lead on," she said, smiling at the two of them as another portal tore into existence.

❖

Jerico marched beside Kaide and Bellok as they kept ahead of the wildfire. Behind them burned the bodies of both friend and foe, for they could not spare the energy to carry them, nor the time to bury them, so in fire they went to their gods.

"They come without horses," Jerico said, nodding toward the approach of Sir Gregane's vanguard.

"Then I am of no more use," Bellok said.

"You have proven yourself to have a thousand uses," Kaide said, smacking his friend on the shoulder. "Don't discount yourself yet."

"Startling horses is a simple cantrip, Kaide. We have no more firestones, and I have gone too long without rest. I doubt I could slay a rabbit if it sat still long enough for me to cast."

All around them marched the rest of the bandits, few of whom Jerico knew. They'd lost a third when the horses came crashing in, and would have lost far more if it hadn't been for Bellok letting out whistle after strange whistle, confusing the mounts and sending them crashing into each other. Jerico's mace was caked with blood, and he knew the killing was far from over.

"What do we do?" he asked Kaide as they marched. "We cannot hold lines against them. The two of us may kill twenty, thirty before going down, but the rest?"

"I know," Kaide said, keeping his voice low. "I'd hoped the fire would spread much faster, but it seems the very weather turns against us. But what choice do we have?"

Jerico eyed the forest, knowing potential safety hid within.

"We run," he said. "Your men lack armor, and our chasers are burdened. If we reach Arthur's men, we stand a chance."

"Sounds like the pally wants to be a coward," said Adam, who had lurked behind them without saying anything to alert them to his presence.

"Who says we should be running?" asked Griff beside him. He grinned despite the wicked cut across his face, which had slashed off a portion of his nose.

"We run to a better location," Jerico said. Though his whole body ached, he smiled. "And then we fight."

"There," Kaide said, pointing to a far portion of the forest. "We'll make it, so long as Gregane doesn't throw any soldiers our way to cut us off."

"He does, we'll crash right on through," Jerico said. "And with my shield leading the way. Give the order, Kaide."

The bandit leader looked to his men, and he mustered one last bit of energy and bravado.

"We run!" he shouted. "Ignore those bastards, and leave their clanking asses in our dust! We go to meet with Arthur. With us at his side, we can hold off soldiers from dawn to dusk, and spill their blood a thousand times more than our own!"

They cheered. Jerico led the way, conditioned to run in his armor for long periods of time. At first the vanguard tensed, thinking them charging, but then they saw the angle was wrong. He heard them cry out, and then the chase was on.

"Run!" Jerico shouted when he could spare the breath. He'd put his shield onto his back, but he pulled it off and stopped, lifting it high so that the stragglers might see its light. "Run, my friends, for the life of all you love, run!"

As its light shone over them, they surged ahead with lifted spirits and refreshed legs. Jerico returned the shield to his back, sparing a glance backward and wishing he hadn't. The soldiers were less than a hundred yards behind and gaining ground. Kaide's men had fought to their last breath to survive the initial charge of the knights. Unburdened or not, they were tired, and struggled to keep pace.

Up ahead, the forest seemed so very far away.

"Come," Jerico said, grabbing one man by the arm and tugging him along. "One foot after another, now move!"

The man staggered, more pulled than running. Jerico caught up to two more, and he saw blood on them. He admired their courage, and was torn on what to do. He grabbed the arm of a second, knowing that the other he did not choose was doomed to death.

"My Ashhur take you," he said. The man had no anger in his eyes, only fear, and that look haunted Jerico as he rushed along. He saw one man stumble, and he let go of the first and reached down to help the second. Up ahead, Kaide shouted for them to run, but so many were tired and wounded. Jerico could do no more. Begging Ashhur for his understanding, he at last grabbed the arm of another injured man who collapsed, flung him onto his back, and ran. When those around him fell behind, or stumbled, he left them to their fate, to live or die by their own strength. Every time he saw it, though, he felt another stab in his gut.

They were almost to the forest when a squad of men finally noticed their approach. They turned and formed a line, what few shields they had taking up the front. Kaide shifted them further away, and Gregane's troops hurried to match. Behind them, the vanguard slowed, both to fight the stragglers as well as catch their breath, for as Jerico had hoped, they were more used to riding into battle, and their heavy armor had finally taken its toll.

Not that he felt that much better himself, but despite that, he shoved to the front, where Kaide ran with his dirks drawn.

"Crash through," Kaide said, not even slowing.

"That or death," Jerico said, pulling his shield off his back. He held it above his head, letting friend and foe know his approach.

"For Ashhur!" he cried, and it echoed across the gulch, louder than even the fire. The light of his shield flared, and he slammed into the line. Blades clanked off his armor, no one able to score a solid hit because of the light. Jerico twisted and swung, smashing through while knocking over everyone near. Behind him, the rest of the bandits surged, forcing through the gap. Jerico remained, like a wedge holding up a heavy stone. Even Kaide hurried through, but only after slashing open the throats of nearby soldiers to satisfy his bloodlust.

When at last Sebastian's troops recovered from the brutal assault, Jerico again turned to run. He felt blows striking him, and something sharp slashed against his face, but he endured. Crying out the name of his god, he slammed a man aside with his shield, parried a chop, and then reached open ground. He ran until he found the ditch, and just barely managed to slow himself so he didn't break his legs in the sudden drop. He more rolled than climbed down, then accepted Adam's waiting arms pulling him up.

"How many?" Jerico asked, looking back.

"Half," Kaide said, looking through the trees at where his friends fought and died. Jerico whispered them a prayer, then fell to his knees to recover his breath.

"They'll charge soon," Bellok said. He leaned against a tree, and he sounded winded from the run. "I say we get our asses out of here."

"We don't run," Kaide said, glaring at the remaining hundred men at his command. "Not now. Not when victory still remains."

"Victory," Jerico muttered, looking toward where Arthur's men stood in defense far down the ditch. He could only barely see them, but they still looked terribly outnumbered.

"You held off legions of wolf-men with mere villagers," Kaide said, turning on him. "Don't you lose hope on me now. Lift that damn shield of yours. Let my men see you still stand!"

Though his side ached, and his legs felt on fire, he stood and held his shield high.

"None pass," he shouted as loud as his tired lungs could manage. "Not here. Not while my light still shines!"

The men took up the call, and they lifted their own weapons, daring the soldiers to cross the ditch.

Then Gregane's men let out a cry, and the entire army did just that. At their position, Kaide's men were horribly outnumbered, but unlike the rest of the battlefield, the ditch before them remained empty. That quickly changed. Jerico kept his shield low and swung, smashing his mace through helmets and chestplates. The ditch was deep enough that it came up to the assaulters' waists, and they had to abandon all pretense of attacking to climb. The rest of the bandits kicked and shoved, and they beat at hands and arms with their weapons. Body by body they filled the ditch.

"Too many!" Jerico cried as he looked to the sides. Gregane's men were spreading out, going beyond where they could defend.

"No shit," Kaide yelled back, whirling beside him. His two blades were coated with blood. Between dodging the chaotic swings, he'd dip low and knife a man's throat or plunge a dirk through an eye before continuing along. Jerico was far less fancy, but just as efficient. No man gained ground before him. He shoved with his shield, trusted his armor to protect his lower body, and kept his mace moving side to side. The screams of the dying grew. Jerico looked once to his left and saw enemy soldiers climbing up. In less than a minute, they'd be surrounded.

"We can't hold!" he shouted to Kaide as he slammed his shield to the ground, the light momentarily blinding his attackers. "Give the retreat!"

Kaide gritted his teeth, and his attacks took on a new frenzy. They'd been forced to fall back, unable to hold the ditch any longer. Men climbed free, and they stayed back, defending the rest of their forces. Kaide slashed into them, his blades finding every crease, every gap in the armor. Jerico reminded himself to ask who trained him should they all survive. But despite the fury, there was no way he could turn the tide, not by himself. Already he heard cries to their left, of Arthur's troops sounding the retreat.

The battle was lost.

"Go!" Jerico shouted, plunging into the gathered forces. Blows rained down upon him, denting his armor and slashing cuts across his face. He swung his shield in a high arc, slamming away soldiers, and then grabbed Kaide by the shirt. With all his might he flung the man away.

"I said run!" he screamed as all around him the bandits died. They needed no further orders, not from Kaide. Casting aside their weapons, the remaining few fled. Kaide looked to Jerico, and he mouthed a promise the paladin could not hear amid the din. Then he turned and ran. Jerico brought his attention back to the soldiers, who were cheering their victory. Most rushed to assault, with many giving Jerico a wide berth. They wanted the fleeing men, the ones lacking armor and weaponry.

Twenty remained behind, though, surrounding Jerico in a wide circle. They were the furious, the ones who had lost friends to his mace. Jerico braced himself, his shield tucked against his body as he met their stares.

"Victory is yours," he said. "No one else must die."

"Sebastian will want him prisoner," one of the soldiers said, though the rest murmured in disapproval. None seemed ready to attack, for everyone clearly knew the first to attack would die. Jerico kept shifting, letting none see his back for long.

"To the Abyss with what Sebastian wants," said their leader, who cast off his helmet so Jerico could see his glare.

"Too many died at his feet. Drop your mace, paladin, and I will make it merciful."

Jerico grinned

"I'll die with my weapon in hand," he said. "And only if you can best me."

The rest tensed. The attack was soon to come, and would begin with the first blow. Jerico prayed that Ashhur would be kind, and take him into his arms. He braced for the cries of battle.

The cries came, not of victory, but pain. Fire burned a ring around him, keeping him safe. Another blast of flame came in from outside the forest, consuming many of the soldiers. They turned to face their attacker, as did Jerico, whose blood ran cold at what he saw. Approaching the forest was a man in the black robes of Karak, his deathly skin pale in the sunlight. Dim red eyes shone from beneath his hood, which hid all but his bemused smile. A woman was with them, dressed in gray. Two dark paladins walked at his side, one a stranger, and one painfully familiar.

"Darius," Jerico whispered.

"He is mine," the man in black said, pointing to the remaining soldiers. "Go seek the spoils of your war elsewhere."

Despite their fury at his magic, the remaining men knew they could not challenge one who wielded fire with his bare hands. They hurried on, chasing after Kaide. Jerico lifted his shield, his eyes unable to leave Darius. The man had a starved look about him, all traces of his good humor long vanished. Pain was evident in his eyes as he gave Jerico a cold glare. Around Jerico, the fire spread, setting trees aflame. At his feet, though, the grass blackened and died, but did not burn. The heat was heavy, but the smoke rose on the wind, and the fire only burned outward.

"Paladin of Ashhur," shouted the pale man who seemed a priest. "Karak has declared your life forfeit. Meet your executioner."

And then Darius drew his sword. At sight of the dark fire wreathed about its blade, Jerico felt his last vestige of hope die.

17

Darius felt the eyes of everyone upon him as he stepped into the burning forest. Even Karak seemed to watch him, and he prayed he would not disappoint. His faith was strong. He would endure. No matter that Jerico looked to him with such betrayal and sadness that it rent a hole in his heart. No matter that he felt fury at the entire circumstances thrusting them into such a battle. Only Karak's will mattered, and Karak's desire was plain, simple.

"I will not ask for forgiveness," Darius said as he lifted his sword with both hands and adopted an offensive stance. "Not for this. You are to die, Jerico. My god demands it."

For a brief moment, the old Jerico surfaced, a half-smile stretching at his face.

"Then tell him no."

Darius grinned, though he felt no humor.

"Not this time. I have rejected him once, and was rejected in turn. Not again. You are a plague upon this world, a false light that must be extinguished. Dezrel was not made in your image. Ashhur's hope is a hope of fools and peasants. Karak is truth. The wretched, the broken, the selfish, the weak ... they will burn in fire. My fire."

He swung, and it seemed his entire world slowed to a crawl. His sword struck Jerico's shield, two lights intertwining, the dark and light bursting together in violent sparks that showered the ground. Darius felt a spike of pain from the contact, but Jerico felt it as well. Both staggered back, breathing heavily.

"I won't break," Jerico said, repositioning his shield. "You know that."

"I know you're a fool." He swung again, trying to shatter Jerico as if he were a stone. Sword and shield connected, and the shockwave of it echoed throughout the forest. "I know my faith is stronger. I will break you. I have no choice!"

At his third swing, Jerico parried it aside with his mace and then lunged, his shield leading. Darius screamed at the painful light. Never before had it made his eyes ache so. He turned away and rolled, avoiding a swing from the mace. Spinning on his knees, he kicked to his feet, stabbing. Jerico shifted to the side, narrowly avoiding an impaling.

"No choice?" Jerico cried, stepping back as Darius swung wildly. "Is that what you tell yourself? You are no slave, Darius, no puppet. I was your friend, damn it, remember that!"

"Friend?" Darius asked as their weapons connected. When Jerico tried to shove forward with his shield, Darius was ready. He pulled back and struck it with his blade, the dark fire flaring. They both felt the pain, but Darius knew his blows were raining down ever harder, Karak's strength flooding his veins. The other paladin staggered deeper into the forest. The red light of the fire shone upon them, and in the glow Darius felt himself returned to the Abyss, fulfilling his visions.

"Friend," Jerico gasped, stumbling onto one knee before quickly standing.

"I gave my life for you," Darius said. "I sacrificed everything, even my faith, for you. And what do I find? You leading a rebellion, sowing chaos throughout the

North. At the side of bandits? Rebels? I have suffered every day since, cast off, abandoned, tortured ... and I see it was for nothing. You worship a lie. Too long I accepted it, treated you as an equal. But you're not. You're nothing, and at last I see it ... friend."

Jerico shook his head, at last showing despair.

"You can't believe that," he said quietly.

"By my actions, my proof."

Darius swung, only to have Jerico block. The metal of his mace groaned, but held. Jerico shoved it aside, then shifted so his shield shone its light directly into his eyes. Darius fell back, swinging wildly to keep the other paladin at bay.

"Where were you when I suffered in prison?" he cried. "Where was Ashhur when Velixar took the lives of his faithful? Where were either of you as I butchered that family? He has abandoned this world, abandoned us all! Look at you, last of his kind. What lies can you offer? What hope can you possibly believe in? Tell me why ... tell me why I wasn't stopped?"

Jerico remained back, seemingly with no desire to go on the offensive. The sadness on his face only grew with every word Darius spoke, and for whatever reason, that infuriated him further. Darius stepped in and swung, crying out the name of his god. The fire on his blade consumed it fully, and a word came to his lips, its meaning unknown to him.

"Felholad!" he screamed. The very metal of his blade vanished, nothing but the burning will of his god. It struck Jerico's shield with the sound of thunder. Bright light flared, but Darius's fire sucked it in and defeated it. Jerico flew back several feet before hitting a tree, his head smacking against it hard enough to leave a smear of blood. He slumped to his knees, remaining upright only by leaning his weight on his fists. Blood trickled down his neck and dripped to the scorched grass.

Darius held his blade high, clutching it with both hands as he towered over his defeated opponent.

"Karak's judgment," he whispered.

"Stand with me," Jerico said, and he looked up without any anger, any malice, only disappointment. "Remember, Darius. Stand with me."

The words Jerico had said during the fight against the wolf-men. Side by side, they'd fought, bled, and been ready to die. And so they had, making their stand against the chaos of the world. It didn't matter Darius had failed to protect his charges, that his lack of strength had doomed many. Jerico had understood, and called him to fight without ever casting blame or judgment.

Side by side.

The fire of his blade, fueled by his hatred, his anguish, his certainty, could no longer be sustained. It dwindled away, still bright, but no longer the Felholad it had become. In that brief moment, Darius felt terrified to be once more alone, abandoned, a failure to the vision he'd seen. In that brief moment, Jerico lunged to his feet, his mace swinging. Darius was too slow to block, only partially deflecting the strike. The mace struck the side of his head, the flanged edges tearing into his skin. Blood spilled, and he collapsed from the blow as his sight blurred. His hands felt strange to him, and the sword slipped to the ground. Tears in his eyes, he saw the fire fade completely.

More than anything, he felt alone. On his knees, he looked up at Jerico, who stood with the mace at ready.

"Do it," he said. "Kill me. Gods help me, you don't know what I've done. I can be this no longer."

Jerico hesitated, and for some reason that hesitation filled Darius with fury.

"I said do it!" he screamed. "Coward! I'll not be judged!"

Instead Jerico flung his mace to the ground, shifted his shield onto his back, and offered his hand. Darius stared at it, unbelieving.

"Take it, and stand," said Jerico.

"Why?" Darius asked.

"Because I need to believe you aren't lost to me, otherwise I might as well throw down my shield and join you in death. Now stand."

Darius felt Velixar's words searing through his mind. He thought of the massacred villagers, of the horrors at Durham. He felt guilt crushing him, denied for so long by a certainty of faith he no longer held. Through it all, one thing echoed over everything: Velixar's own words now turned against him.

Darius looked to Jerico's offered hand, and a face containing no anger, no blame, only forgiveness.

"What this world needs," he whispered.

He took it and stood. Jerico embraced him, and he laughed.

"Ashhur be praised," he said, grinning. "I thought you were going to take my head off."

"I almost did."

Together they looked through the fire, to where Velixar waited. They could see the barest hint of the group, so deep into the forest they had gone during their fight.

"We have to run," Jerico said, nodding the other way. "Sebastian's army will come back to find us soon."

"No," Darius said, glancing at his sword. "No running. Those out there know your name. They'll hunt you forever, and me as well. Let us end this now."

Jerico touched the back of his head, and he winced at the pain. Darius felt guilty for it, but he laughed anyway and smacked Jerico across the shoulder. For whatever reason, even at the prospect of facing down Velixar, he felt almost giddy. He had always expected one of two fates to befall him, either torturing in the Abyss, or being tortured. Somehow he had found a third fate, and it was at Jerico's side.

"If you say we must, then we must," Jerico said, readying his shield and mace. "Let's go."

"Wait," Darius said, unable to control his grin. "I have an idea."

⋈

Valessa felt disappointed to see Darius emerge from the forest into daylight. She'd hoped the other paladin might kill him, and as a failure he'd go to Karak to beg for mercy, mercy he would not receive. Instead he walked with blood on his armor, and his sword sheathed across his back.

"Karak be praised," Velixar said. "He is dead?"

Darius said nothing, only walked silently toward the prophet. Something about the look in his eyes worried Valessa, so much that she found herself itching to draw her daggers. He looked healthier, relieved. Of course, she thought. He'd defeated the burden placed upon him. With Jerico dead, his reparations with Karak were complete. Such a damn shame.

"Is he dead?" Velixar asked again, a note of worry in his voice, as if he too noticed the change. Darius kept calm, his face betraying nothing. He moved between the three, past Velixar, but the prophet reached out and grabbed him by the shoulder. Mallak tensed, also sensing the strange feeling in the air.

"Darius," Velixar said. "Draw your sword."

Darius obeyed, a hint of a smile finally showing on his lips. He drew, and Valessa froze at the shock of what she saw.

Blue light shone across the edges of the blade. So stunned was she, she could only watch as Darius continued the smooth drawing motion into a swing right for Velixar's neck. The sword cut cloth and struck the prophet's pale skin. For a moment it seemed it would do nothing, but the blue light flared stronger, and then the blade passed right on through. Velixar's body burst into dust; his eyes melted into fire. He let out a single cry before he died, a denial against failing, a refusal to accept the death befalling him. Then he was silent.

"Betrayer!" Mallak cried, drawing his sword in time to block Darius's follow-up swing. Their blades connected, showering sparks. The dark fire wreathing Mallak's sword was far greater, and with ease he pushed Darius back. "You will burn for eternity for such cowardice!"

Valessa could not believe her luck. The damned prophet was gone, and here was Darius deserving every bit of pain she could deliver. Karak must have smiled upon her. She watched as the two paladins exchanged swings, with Darius clearly the inferior in strength and passably equal in skill. When she saw an opening, his back completely to her, she tensed her legs to lunge. Searing pain flooded her back before she could, and then she found herself flying through the air. Tucking her shoulder, she rolled, then spun so she might dig her heels into the dirt to halt her momentum.

Chasing after her was Jerico with that damned shield of his. Worse, he was apologizing.

"Sorry," he said, carefully approaching. "Don't like attacking opponents unaware."

"Consider me aware," she said, twirling her daggers in her hands. One opening ... just one opening ...

He lifted his mace to strike, and she went for it, one blade jamming inward to lock his shield out of place, the other thrusting for the gap in his armor at the armpit. Numbing pain jolted into her hand as her dagger hit the shield, but she forced herself on. Her other dagger sliced into flesh, and then she whirled, avoiding the downward chop of his mace. The paladin let out a cry, and it was music to her ears. Continuing her spin, she stayed close, and her daggers stabbed for a crease just above his shoulder.

"I have no problem stabbing a man in the back," she said through clenched teeth as Jerico's body reacted on instinct, arching his upper half toward her. She twisted the dagger, locking his right arm from striking at her with his mace.

"How could you kill Claire?" she asked, still pressed tight against him. "You, a slow, dim-witted fool? She was worlds beyond you."

"Because I ... have ... friends."

Jerico ducked, and Darius's elbow caught her full in the face. Her training kicked in, and Valessa rolled with it to minimize the damage, leaving one of her two daggers still embedded in Jerico's shoulder. When she returned to her feet, the next few seconds were a jumbled blur. Her eyes watered from the hit, and the throbbing in her head seemed to make everything a haze. Jerico fell to one side, still bleeding. Instead of pressing the attack on her, Darius spun, flinging his weapon up to block Mallak's attack, who was far from beaten. Mallak, it seemed, had tried to kill Jerico while he lay helpless. As Valessa lunged to help, Jerico rolled to his knees and lifted his shield. Its light shone upon her, and already weakened, she struggled to push onward. It felt as if her every movement was through ice water. Jerico met her ineffective attack with that damn shield of his. Her whole body pressed against it, but she could only cry out in agony. Never before had she felt such pain.

Valessa hit the ground, her only conscious thought that of the ringing in her ears. As if from someone else's body, she watched the battle end. Jerico turned his shield back to Mallak, joining the traitor Darius's side. Mallak, seemingly realizing he had to end the fight quickly now that he was outnumbered, assaulted the wounded Jerico with all his might. The fire of his blade flared, and he struck with awesome fury. Jerico's shield weathered the blows, though he cried out in pain all the while. But Darius was there, and he took the opening before him. Valessa silently shrieked as the traitor thrust his blade through a crease in Mallak's armor, and then twisted the handle. Blood gushed from Mallak's side, and when he coughed, more spilled across his lips and neck. He fell.

"Help me," Valessa whispered, struggling to stand. It was as if her limbs had suddenly stopped taking orders. "Please, Karak, help me ..."

Jerico fell to one knee, and he screamed when Darius yanked out the dagger she had lodged into his shoulder. Whatever satisfaction she might have felt meant nothing knowing he would survive. So many dead, and all their fault ... all their fault.

"Karak," she breathed. "I am your darkness. I am your shadow. Do not abandon me. Not now."

The two paladins turned their attention to her, and there was no misunderstanding the look in Darius's eyes as he approached.

"Don't," she heard Jerico say, and she felt fury at any false sympathy he might show. Darius refused to listen.

"I'm sending her to her god," said the traitor. "I know what she is, what she is capable of. The world is better this way."

"I will hunt you," Valessa said to him, even as tears welled in her eyes. "Even to the Abyss."

The traitor knelt beside her, and he touched her face with a hand even as the other lifted his sword so the point rested against her throat.

"I will never feel the Abyss's flames," he said. "Don't you see, sister? I'm Karak's champion no longer."

"Darius!" cried Jerico.

He hesitated, and that was enough for her. With the last of her strength, she flung herself onto his blade. The metal pierced flesh, her whole body retched, and then she felt fire burning.

Jerico and Darius stood over the bodies, and they watched as Valessa's corpse was consumed by a dark fire.

"I've never seen such a thing," Darius said, watching until she was all but ash.

"I think we've seen more than few firsts today," Jerico said, and he grinned despite the pain and blood that trickled down the inside of his armor. With his good arm, he gestured to where Gregane's army had pushed into the forest in chase of Lord Arthur's men.

"I think we should get out of here," he said, chuckling despite the pain it caused. "At some point they're going to come back, and I doubt they'll be happy with us."

"Where do we go?" Darius asked as he came over to inspect his wounds.

"Later," Jerico said, pushing him back. "I've survived worse. And where should we go? You're an outlaw now, as much as I."

Darius looked to the forest.

"I spoke with Sebastian," he said. "I've seen how his mind works. If Arthur is alive, we need to help him. It only seems right, given the mess I helped cause here in the North."

"Plenty my fault, too," Jerico said, and he leaned on Darius to remain standing. "Let's put Gregane's army far behind us. I know a place we can hide."

Epilogue

"You are certain?" Sir Robert Godley asked as he leaned back in his wooden chair, which creaked from his weight.

"Sure as I am of anything in this world," said Jeremy Hangfield, who stood with his hands clasped behind his back, the chosen spokesmen for the people of Durham.

"And you have witnesses who will swear to this?"

"Over a hundred," Jeremy said. "This was something we'll never forget. We'll say it until our graves, or the king brings us justice."

"Go," Robert said, dismissing him. "I promise you an answer by tomorrow."

The man bowed and left Robert to be alone with his most trusted friend, Daniel Coldmine, in his room in the Blood Tower.

"This is bad," Daniel said.

"I gathered as much."

"No, you don't understand." Daniel leaned on the desk with both hands, and he looked out the window to the distant wildlands of the Wedge. "A paladin of Karak? We can't make enemies with the Stronghold. You know damn well how favored his priests are in the capital."

"But that many witnesses ..."

"They'll mean nothing, and you know it. All their lives are a pile of shit in the eyes of anyone outside the North."

Robert crossed his arms and forced himself to bite his tongue. He knew there were good people in the capital, but Daniel was right. Given the current balance of power, they would be making enemies of those who controlled the mind and heart of the king.

"What is it you think I should do?" he asked.

"Bring him in for questioning," Daniel said, turning to him. "Play it safe. Either that, or give him over to the Stronghold and let them handle the matter."

Robert scratched at his chin, then shook his head.

"No. I'm tired of these games, Daniel. The whole North is in chaos because of those two Hemman brothers, and the king already loathes my name. He'll leave me to settle this on my own, and settle it I will. I want proclamations given to every single village along the Gihon, and for them to send riders west until they reach the sea announcing the same. The dark paladin known as Darius shall be executed on sight, without trial or capture. Offer the largest reward we can afford. A hundred people watched him burn their village to the ground, a village I helped save! If he'll destroy what all our good men died for, then we'll destroy him, and to the Abyss with what the Stronghold might think."

"Are those your orders?" Daniel asked.

"They are," said Robert. "And I expect them carried out."

Daniel saluted.

"You're thrusting fire at a hornet's nest," he said. "But I'll trust you."

He left the room, and once alone, Robert swore up a storm.

"Damn you, Darius," he said, slamming a fist against the top of his desk. "How could you do such a thing? How?"

He would receive no answers, for he wanted none. The entire North would descend upon him, and if the world were just, Darius would receive the punishment he deserved. And if Karak had a problem with that ...

"I'm afraid of no gods," Robert said. "Not Ashhur. Not Karak. None of you."

He thought of the corpses strewn across Durham's streets, of what the Stronghold's reaction might be, and then poured himself a drink to help make some truth of that statement.

※◈※

Valessa thought she went to her god, to join her deity in the Abyss, but something was wrong. The image of Darius refused to fade. Fire burned across her flesh, but she saw no darkness, just the face of a man who had turned against everything she stood for. Her body felt strange, full of pain but without any definitive source. At last Darius's face broke like shards of glass, and she saw darkness. Within that darkness, a lion roared.

Not yet, she heard a voice say, the words flooding her existence with cold terror.

And then she was plummeting downward, feeling wind blasting against her hard enough to steal away her breath ... if she was still breathing. When she hit, she screamed, and all at once her senses returned to her. The world was dark, and high above glittered a field of stars. She felt no sensations of heat, or cold. All she felt was pain, a constant ache from every part of her pale, naked body. Looking about, she realized she was beyond the Gulch, instead at the distant shrine where she had met Karak's prophet.

When she took a step, she fell. Forcing herself back to her feet, she took another, this time watching her naked body to see what betrayed her.

When she moved, her body lost all color, texture, and became a swirl of shadow.

You have your most heartfelt desire, that cold voice spoke once more. *Find him. Kill him. I will not wait for my prophet's return to bring punishment to my most unfaithful servant.*

"As you wish," Valessa whispered to the stars. Near where she awoke, she saw her daggers lying there, as if calling out to her. When she brought them into her hands, they swirled with darkness and power.

"Thank you," she prayed, and she would have cried if her body remained capable of tears. "Thank you so much."

Her heart's greatest desire.

At her hands, Darius would die.

Note from the Author:

It's hard to describe just how difficult this book was to write.

I mean, it shouldn't have been. Bringing back recurring characters always makes things easier than starting from scratch. In terms of length, Clash of Faiths isn't particularly long. Heck, it even featured Velixar prominently, who makes every scene I write so much easier and enjoyable. So what was so difficult?

I've done scenes where Velixar tries to tear down a paladin before (notably in Shadows of Grace, with delicious scenes between him and Jerico). But this time, it wasn't someone fighting against him, proving him wrong. It was someone accepting him. It was someone willing to believe, if only for a moment, that he might be right. That the story went down a dark road for awhile after that doesn't surprise me in the slightest. Jerico's words very much echoed my own, so much I wonder if Darius's salvation was a necessity for myself. Accompanied by Jerico's own failures and struggles, this whole novel was an uphill climb. I'm glad they've reached the top, and are now side by side (for however long). They've got some work to do.

Not sure when I'll be back for paladins #3, though it is pretty clear that I will be soon. Darius and Jerico are not yet done, and I have a sneaking suspicion Darius will have a book of his own. And Valessa...ah Valessa, I plan on having so much fun with you. I say that in an author sense, not any weird, creepy...moving on. More paladins, but not yet. I've got plenty of readers wanting me to finish up Haern's story in the Shadowdance Trilogy, so that's next on the project list. Hopefully not too long after, I can see how well Darius takes to a new set of morals and beliefs. I have a feeling it won't be easy.

As always, thanks for making it to the end. I hope you enjoyed yourself immensely, and if you didn't, I apologize and promise to do better next time. If you'd like some updates, swing by www.facebook.com/thehalforcs or ddalglish.com. I try to keep them both current on what I'm doing. Also, feel free to email me at ddalglish@yahoo.com and I'll try to respond promptly. One last big thanks to all of you who have been writing reviews, recommending to friends, groups, and on message boards. You've kept me going, and helped me entertain countless others. It's still just me, flinging my stories to the world and hoping readers give it life. I couldn't, nor wouldn't, do this without you. Thank you.

David Dalglish
July 23, 2011

4485334R00139

Printed in Great Britain
by Amazon.co.uk, Ltd.,
Marston Gate.